AFTER SYLVIA

AFTER SYLVIA

ALAN CUMYN

A GROUNDWOOD BOOK

DOUGLAS & McINTYRE

TORONTO VANCOUVER BERKELEY

Groundwood Books / Douglas & McIntyre
720 Bathurst Street, Suite 500, Toronto, Ontario M5S 2R4
Distributed in the USA by Publishers Group West
1700 Fourth Street, Berkeley, CA 94710

We acknowledge for their financial support of our publishing program the Canada Council for the Arts, the Government of Canada through the Book Publishing Industry Development Program (BPIDP), the Ontario Arts Council and the Government of Ontario through the Ontario Media Development Corporation's Ontario Book Initiative.

ONTARIO ARTS COUNCIL
CONSEIL DES ARTS DE L'ONTARIO

National Library of Canada Cataloguing in Publication Data
Cumyn, Alan
After Sylvia / by Alan Cumyn
ISBN 0-88899-612-8 (bound).–ISBN 0-88899-646-2 (pbk.)
I. Title.
PS8555.U489A9 2004   jC813'.54   C2004-902716-6

Cover illustration by Sami Suomalainen
Design by Michael Solomon
Printed and bound in Canada

For Anna and Gwen

TABLE OF CONTENTS

THE BIRDS

OWEN Skye could not sleep. He lay in the dark in the middle of the big bed that he shared with his brothers, Andy and Leonard. It was early September, the night before the first day of school, but the wind that shivered the walls threatened to blow everything into winter.

Summer holidays were ending! The fact of it had loomed over everything for the past several days, and the boys had raced to all the great places — to Dead Man's Hill, to the river, the woods, the haunted house and the railroad tracks — in an effort to squeeze the last drops of adventure from the season.

Now summer was draining away. Owen stared at the ceiling of the attic bedroom and racked his brain trying to think of something, anything, to delay the dreadful start of school.

"What about the crystal radio?" he whispered.

"Shhh!" Leonard said. "It's time for sleep!" He was the youngest and so knew the least about the horrors of education.

"We haven't tried the crystal radio in ages," Owen insisted. Last winter — it seemed like years ago — the boys had used the set to intercept messages from alien spacecraft.

"The radio's been put away," Andy said in a tired voice. Normally he would have been the one to suggest hauling it out in a situation like this, but even he seemed resigned to the end of the season.

"I know where it is," Owen said. It was in a shoe box in the corner of their closet.

Owen slept in the middle, so to get out he had to crawl over Leonard and then creep to the closet in the darkness. The wooden floor was cold on his toes, and the closet door creaked badly when he opened it. Dust from the shoe box made him sneeze twice.

"You three go to sleep!" the boys' father, Horace, shouted from downstairs, and Owen held his breath.

On the next sneeze Owen plugged his nose and swallowed the explosion, popping his ears painfully. But there was no more comment from downstairs, so he reached forward until his fingers felt the hard corners of the shoe box. He took it and slowly, carefully, crawled around the bed to the window. When he pulled off the lid, out sprang a tangled mess of antenna wire. Owen pulled it clear in handfuls, then lifted out the crystal radio set itself.

It was a thing of beauty. It had a varnished wooden base with a large metal coil on the side and even more brass knobs than Owen knew what to do with.

Normally Andy operated it. Owen wasn't sure how to attach the antenna wire, which was a fairly new addition. He had seen Andy hook an end of wire around one of the brass knobs and then run the rest over the curtain rod and across to the light switch near the door. But which knob should Owen attach it to? And would he be able to untangle the wire enough to reach the switch?

Owen wanted to ask Andy for advice, but the older boy was pretending to sleep now, snoring and snorting even louder than usual. So Owen chose one knob at random on the set, attached an end of wire and pulled the rest of the tangle as far as he could over the curtain rod. He climbed on a chair and looped part of it around the overhead light, then ran the rest to the sailing ship lamp that was mounted on the wall a few feet above the boys' bed.

"It won't work like that," Andy muttered between fake snores.

"How do you know?" Owen said.

"It just won't."

Owen ignored him and returned to the radio set. There was dead silence from the tiny speaker. Outside, the wind was racing thin gray clouds across the dark sky. For a moment Owen thought he heard low rattles and indistinct stutters, but it was Leonard tossing in bed and creaking the old frame.

"Try adjusting the clip," Andy whispered. "You can move it along the coil."

Owen peered at the complicated instrument until finally, in the shadows, he could just make out the clip that Andy had mentioned. It was a wire from the speaker that was attached to one of the coils, and Owen saw that it could be unclipped and moved to a different coil.

As soon as Owen moved the clip, it sounded like birds had flown into the room.

"What's that?" Leonard moaned. "I'm trying to get to sleep!"

"It's birds," Owen said. "Birds on the radio!"

Many different birds, it seemed. Some of them warbled and others trilled. There were high, looping calls and soft, burbly murmurs like stream water rushing over stones.

In a few seconds Andy was beside him, ears trained on the soft noises, and then Leonard, too, poked his head close to the little speaker.

The sound was low but distinct. Andy told Owen that if he hooked up the battery, they could boost the speaker power and hear better. But the battery didn't seem to be in the box.

"Why would birds be on the radio?" Owen asked.

"Maybe they took over the station," Leonard said.

"Don't be ridiculous," Andy said. "Birds can't take over a station!"

"Why not?" Leonard asked. "They take over trees. They take over telephone poles. We have no idea what they're talking about."

Owen looked outside to see if masses of birds were whirling through the sky, preparing to occupy the house. But the sky was clear.

"Those birds sound familiar," Leonard said.

"Familiar!" Andy said, twisting the word to make it seem ridiculous. "Friends of yours? Birds that you've met?"

"I don't know," Leonard said cautiously. "It's just that… "

The birds stopped singing on the radio then and Owen heard voices, very low. One of them was an announcer saying, "That was a taste of nature from one of the best bird-whistlers in the county." And the other…

"That's Uncle Lorne!" Owen blurted, and the brothers looked at one another in amazement.

Then the house shook with the sound of heavy feet on the stairs, and all three boys dove for the bed together. They were still writhing when their father pushed open the door, and a sudden shaft of light from the hall split the room.

"What are you three up to?" Horace asked darkly.

Owen clung to his brothers in tense, unbreathing stillness.

"Is there a bird in here?" Horace asked then.

The crystal radio had started throbbing again.

Owen sat up and announced, "It's Uncle

Lorne!" But Andy instantly pulled him back down.

"What are you talking about?" Horace asked, stepping farther into the room.

Owen saw him in a blurry way, through half-clenched eyes. Horace was not normally an angry father, but lately he could blow into a sudden storm over little things — a broken window, spilled ketchup, a story on the news.

Just then the bird noises surged in volume, and Owen wondered if Andy had suddenly found and hooked up the battery after all.

"It is birds!" Horace said. He walked over to the window to look out, but bumped into the tangle of antenna wires instead.

"Careful!" Owen said, sitting up now and not pretending to be asleep at all. "It's Uncle Lorne on the crystal radio."

Horace freed himself from the jumble of wires and put a big ear close to the puny speaker.

"How do you turn this thing up?" he asked.

So Andy rummaged through the back of the closet and brought out his big battery. When he hooked up the terminals, the whistling filled the room like a whole flock.

"It is Lorne!" Horace said. "I haven't heard him whistle like that in years." Then he, too, started to whistle, though his music wasn't full and convincing like Lorne's.

In a few minutes the boys' mother blew into the room.

"What's going on?" Margaret demanded. "Why is everyone up? School starts tomorrow! Back to bed *now*!" She had such snap to her voice that they all jumped. But only Horace moved away from the radio.

"It's Lorne," Horace said in the soft voice he used to try to calm her.

"Whistling like a bunch of birds!" Owen declared.

"Who?" Margaret asked, and she walked straight into the antenna wire.

Then she screamed, and in the confusion pulled the sailing ship lamp off the wall and onto the bed where the boys had been just moments before. The lightbulb smashed against the bed frame and burning sparks shot into the air and filled the room with angry, choking smoke.

"Hands off! Those wires are live!" Horace commanded, and he pushed Margaret to safety.

"Stay where you are!" He turned to the boys, who were trapped behind the electrified antenna wire and the smoking wreck of the sailing ship lamp. "Don't move an inch! Understand?"

"Yes, sir," Andy said immediately, for them all. It was a direct order and Owen felt himself stiffening as if standing at attention. The window was behind them and there really wasn't anywhere they *could* go. The antenna wire, ominously crackling, was looped over the curtain rod just above their heads, and the burning line to the bed cut off their escape.

In a second Horace was gone from the room.

Leonard started to whimper, and Margaret told him to stay very still.

"You'll be all right," she said, but her voice didn't sound all right. It sounded like a tree about to crack in a storm.

The boys' blanket was smoking badly now, and Owen could barely see his mother standing beyond the wires. It was hard not to cough, and his eyes smarted. Leonard started to wriggle beside him and came dangerously close to touching the wire.

"Open the window so you can breathe better,"

Margaret said tensely. "Andy, you know how to do it. Just turn in your place."

Andy and Owen moved together, and in a moment they had the window open. It wasn't so difficult as long as they didn't panic. Owen had a good seven inches between him and electrocution.

But with the window open all the smoke rushed into the boys' faces, and soon the three of them were coughing even worse than before.

"Stay calm! Don't move!" Margaret screamed at them. She seemed helpless over there in the smoke.

How suddenly everything had changed, Owen thought. Just a few moments ago they had been listening to bird songs on the radio.

Owen looked out the window. He had often imagined pulling himself out onto the ledge and reaching across to the drainpipe that might hold a boy his size but then again might not. Yet he had never climbed down a drainpipe before. Tree limbs, yes, but not drainpipes. He might lose his grip, plunge to the ground and break his neck, or worse.

Or worse.

Owen wondered where his father had gone. In the middle of an emergency he had just run away. And the smoke was mounting. They were all going to choke to death standing where they were.

One boy had to climb down the drainpipe.

It should have been Andy, because he was the oldest, strongest, bravest, and by far the best climber. But Andy was frozen, standing still right where he'd been ordered by their mother, who clearly didn't understand the full danger of the situation.

And so, Owen realized, they were all going to die.

Unless he did something.

He pulled himself out the window onto the ledge and gripped with the edges of his toes. It was so cold! He reached as far as he could and hit nothing but empty air. Then at last he felt the wooden side of the house, which he gripped as if his life depended on it. And it did! All their lives, now, depended on his fingers finding the old drainpipe.

It was too far!

He had to untighten his toes and move his reluctant feet along the ledge, closer, closer. Every step was agony. His body was clenched in fear, and the simplest thing — straightening his arm — felt impossible.

"What are you doing?" Andy yelled to him from inside.

Owen reached the drainpipe at last. He knew if he hesitated even slightly he'd never be able to do it, so he grabbed and swung immediately.

For a moment he felt his body suspended in blackness with nothing beneath him, his fingers clutched to the flimsiest tin piping. Then his toes were banging wildly against the house until they, too, gripped the groaning drainpipe, and he was completely free of the ledge, like a worm clutching a leaf in a windstorm.

"Mom says get back in here right now!" Andy shouted.

Too late! Owen was suspended far above the earth, being held up by something that had no right to support his weight. Consumed with the effort to hang on, he found he couldn't speak, much less work his way down to the ground.

"The fire's out!" Andy yelled. "Dad turned off the electricity!"

Margaret's head appeared at the window.

"Owen Skye! Get back in here right now!" she ordered.

He wanted to, very much, but the ledge was a terrible stretch away. It was also slightly above him, for he had fallen a bit in his leap of faith, and his body was reluctant to do anything at the moment that required unclenching.

"I can't," he said in a little voice.

A bracket came loose from the wall then, and the drainpipe groaned. It started to sway away from the window. Owen thrust his bare feet against the wall and somehow stopped the slide.

"Dad's gone to get the ladder!" Andy yelled.

But the more Owen thought about it, the more he realized that Horace would never get the ladder in time. It was in the garage, wedged behind the sawhorse and the wheelbarrow and a rusting baby carriage that had been there when the Skyes had moved in years ago.

The drainpipe swayed even farther. The bracket was only going to last a few more seconds. Horace was probably still looking for a flashlight in the dark to see where the ladder might be.

Why was everything going wrong?

Owen closed his eyes and imagined Sylvia Tull

sitting all the way across the classroom from him as she had in school every year before this one. She was the kind of girl — well, no, she was the only girl — who drove blood up Owen's face with a simple glance, and baked his ears tomato red, and made speech barely possible. He thought of all the hours he had spent imagining an airplane crashing through the window, and how he had planned to spring across the chaos of that moment and throw her under a desk, shield her from disaster with his body.

He knew now what a hopeless fantasy that had been! For here he was, in a moment of great physical danger, and instead of being a superhero he was a worm, too scared to move.

And now Sylvia was gone. Her family had moved to faraway Elgin, and he would never see her again.

Owen reached his foot down an inch or two and lowered himself painfully.

From the direction of the garage he heard the crashing of large things and then his father cursing and calling angrily for Andy to help him find the ladder.

Owen let himself down another inch.

———

He breathed out violently and imagined Sylvia at his funeral, how his brothers would stare at her and not understand anything about who she was and why she was there. But would she even come to his funeral? How would she hear about it? Elgin was miles away, in another world almost. He would never see her again.

Especially if he died in the next few seconds.

Then the drainpipe swayed badly, and Owen felt his hands and feet slide down the side of the house. He thought he was lost, but his ankle struck something that slowed the fall. He reached and wildly grabbed a bracket — a solid one, this time. The top section of the drainpipe came down past his head and smashed onto the ground so far below. But Owen's section was holding!

And the strangest thing happened. Owen looked up at the night sky and saw a dark formation of birds wheeling against the moon that shone through a hole in the clouds. They looped high and turned over, all of them at the same time, and swooped off beyond his vision. It was unspeakably graceful, like Uncle Lorne's whistling — Lorne who was tall and awkward and terribly shy, and who reminded no one of a delicate, beautiful songbird. And yet that was his voice Owen had heard on the radio. And now birds were showing him how easy it was to fly.

Owen couldn't fly, of course, but he could certainly shinny down the rest of the drainpipe if he didn't think about it too much. It was like slipping down the main trunk of the apple tree in the yard or the banister in the hall stairs.

He stood on the ground dizzy and cold and looked up to see the birds. But they were gone, and the house itself seemed unfamiliar in this light and unsteady in the wind, as if it might collapse upon itself suddenly. Owen looked and looked, but it stayed where it was, shivering in the breeze.

And soon he was surrounded again by his mother and father and brothers, all talking at once, like a flock of birds still clacking even after they have escaped an angry dog.

BROKEN EGGS

OWEN came downstairs early the next morning and found Horace alone in the kitchen. Owen sat at the table and glumly watched his father poke the bacon in the big black cast-iron frying pan. It had been hard to sleep, even though Margaret had cleaned up the bed and found the boys a new blanket and left the window wide open. The smell of smoke still clung to Owen's pajamas, and his eyes were red. And it was chilly in the old farmhouse that wasn't really a farmhouse anymore. All the surrounding fields, which Owen could see out the window soaked in cold dew, belonged to other families and were worked by real farmers.

Owen poured himself a glass of orange juice.

"Did you ever think of moving to Elgin?" he asked his father.

"Why would we want to do that?" Horace replied.

"I don't know," Owen said.

"Everything's a lot more expensive in town," Horace said. And then he changed the subject. "Are you nervous about school?" he asked.

"A bit," Owen said.

"I remember getting so upset," Horace said. "Because of the multiplication codes."

"What codes?"

"Well, you know the multiplication *tables*," Horace said.

Owen nodded. He had sweated for months to learn those.

"Well, every year the teachers choose a new multiplication code," Horace said. "They get together in a big, secret meeting in the summertime, and they say, 'Seven times six used to be forty-two, but this year we'll agree to make it forty-seven.'"

"They can't do that!" Owen said in alarm.

"Of course they can. They're teachers. They can do what they want." Horace took a long drink of his coffee and poked the bacon some more with a fork. "They might decide the new multiplication table was last year's answer plus five. Or maybe plus five for even numbers and minus five for odd."

"But why would they do that?" Owen asked.

"Otherwise it would be too easy," Horace said. "If the tables just stayed the same every year, then what would the kids have to learn? The teachers would lose their jobs. Not enough work. The unions are very strong over this."

Horace started on the toast then, and that took all his attention, since the toaster didn't pop on its own anymore and only heated things on one side at a time. Owen was left to ponder the terrible news while Leonard and Andy straggled down the stairs.

Nothing could be counted on anymore, not even the multiplication tables.

When Horace finished the toast he put it in the oven to warm, then turned his attention back to the frying pan. Owen watched as his father scooped the bacon onto a plate, wrapped it in a cloth to soak up the grease and placed the plate in the oven. Then he drained the rest of the grease from the pan into an empty jar, quickly cleaned the remaining grit off the surface and returned a small amount of grease to the pan.

Owen had watched this mysterious process many times. Horace went to the fridge and pulled out six eggs — two for himself and one each for everyone else. In a few minutes, when the pan was again hot enough, he would one-handedly crack and pour each egg, then fire the empty shells into the sink for someone else to clean up.

Horace did nothing in the kitchen at any other time, but he was the king of breakfast.

Owen didn't feel like the king of anything. He tried to think of what he was good at. Andy could conjure adventures out of air and Leonard was smarter than almost any kid his age, but Owen felt like he had no special skill. And the more he thought about it the less comfortable he felt, as if the walls of the kitchen itself were leaning in on him and either he had to grow this instant or he'd be squeezed to death. All through his body he felt an aching wave of nervousness that almost made his skin itch.

And so, on the spur of the moment and before Horace could crack the first shell, Owen stood up and said that he wanted to cook his own egg.

"You *can't* cook your own egg," Horace said irritably. He didn't explain, but Owen understood. It would ruin the schedule. How long would it take to get this family through breakfast if everyone insisted on frying his own egg?

But Margaret, who walked into the kitchen at precisely that moment, said sharply, "Of course he can!" Her hair was bunched up badly on one side of her head — the sign of a wretched night — and even her dressing gown looked rumpled and sore.

"Owen can't cook his own egg!" Andy said.

"Why not?" Margaret asked.

Andy hesitated, then said, "Dad does the breakfast!"

"You boys need to learn how to make your way around a kitchen, too," Margaret said. "Owen is certainly old enough to fry an egg."

Owen thought his brother would argue that he had no right to learn such a thing because Andy hadn't learned it yet and the oldest always did everything first. But Andy stayed quiet and Horace grudgingly said, "All right," and handed Owen an egg.

Owen stepped up to the pan and concentrated on the sharp groove in the side, against which he had seen Horace crack the eggs countless times. It was a quick little motion, mostly a snap of the wrist.

Owen tapped the shell against the side of the pan. Nothing happened.

"Before you crack the egg," Horace said, "you have to be aware of how hot the pan is. If it isn't hot enough, then the egg doesn't cook properly. But if it's too hot —"

Owen again tapped the shell against the edge of the pan, but he couldn't dent it.

"You have to *hit* the thing, Owen! But don't worry about that now. Listen to me! How do you know how hot the pan is? You can tell by the —"

Splat! The shell suddenly collapsed in Owen's fist as he was preparing to hit it against the pan for the third time. Cold, sticky egg guts dripped down the side of the oven and onto the floor.

Andy and Leonard exploded in laughter as Owen stepped back to avoid the mess. Horace barked out, *"Owen!"* and Margaret instantly hovered with a cloth.

"No, no!" Horace said. "If he's going to do eggs, he has to learn to clean up, too." So Margaret gave Owen the cloth and he wiped up the disaster, rinsing the cloth again and again to get off all the egg goop.

Horace handed Owen another egg and said, "Now be careful —"

But before he could finish the thought, Owen had dropped the egg onto the floor between his slippers.

Andy and Leonard couldn't contain themselves. They held onto the breakfast table and howled breathlessly while Owen staggered back to the sink to retrieve the wiping cloth yet again.

"Hurry up!" Horace said. "The pan's getting too hot!" All the time Owen was wiping up the egg, he was conscious of the angry snap and sizzle of the hot grease in the pan.

Finally Horace commanded, "Leave that! You need to put the egg in *now*!"

Owen had to spread his legs to make sure he wasn't stepping in spilled egg. His face was so close to the pan that snapping grease pricked his cheek. He gripped another egg, and with all his concentration tried to make sure he didn't fumble it on the floor, or squeeze it so hard that it shattered in his fingers.

The others were crowding around now to see what new disaster he would achieve.

"Hurry!" Horace urged, so Owen tapped the

egg against the sharp side of the pan. This time it cracked neatly halfway round.

Owen stared at the miracle of it.

"Open it!" Horace said.

Horace always opened his egg with one hand, making it look as easy as unfolding your wings and flying away. But Owen realized now what a complicated thing it was. He dug his thumb and fingers into the crack and felt the shell quiver dangerously.

"Use both hands!" Horace said, but too late. The shell had already collapsed, and egg now dripped down Owen's shaking arm, half into the hissing pan and half onto the stovetop and down the crack where the oven door didn't quite close.

Both of Owen's brothers became writhing, barking beasts, helpless with laughter.

"That's enough!" Horace said, and he grabbed the hot pan with his bare hand and then dropped it, full of searing grease and half-cooked egg, into the sink, where it sizzled in water like the flaming wreck of an airplane hitting the ocean.

The boys had cold cereal for breakfast.

On the way to school Owen wrestled with bad thoughts. Why was the world changing so recklessly? Why were the simplest things turning into disasters? He had tried to set up the crystal radio and almost lost his life having to climb down the drainpipe. Then he had tried to cook his own egg, and the kitchen had turned into a disaster zone. And what was waiting for him at school but a minefield of changed multiplication codes and who knew what else the teachers would dream up?

Why?

Because Sylvia was gone.

Most mornings the boys would start walking to school together. Andy was supposed to make sure they all got to their classrooms safely, and while their mother could see them they usually stayed in a tight clump. They walked with their heads down, unspeaking, carrying their books and their lunch boxes. But as they got farther from the house and its hold on them weakened, the brothers would begin to separate. Andy was a fast walker, Leonard dawdled, scuffing his heels on the gravel road, and Owen kept a middling pace.

So Owen was on his own as he approached the village. He came to the crossroads where his pulse always started to race. Because Sylvia's house — her old house — was just down that road, and in the past Owen would always look to see if she was walking toward him in her blazing orange coat. Sometimes he had timed it perfectly and arrived at the corner just when she did.

He could not keep himself from looking. But instead of a blazing orange coat, all Owen saw was a large, black-haired, slobbery-tongued dog with ears that nearly dragged on the ground and a tail that wouldn't stop wagging.

The dog immediately started running toward him. Something big and awkward was in his mouth — a slimy, muddy rock.

"Hey! Down boy! Stop!" Owen cried, but muddy paws were on his chest, and the dog's wet face — and the rock — were rubbing against his neck.

Owen pushed him away and started walking more quickly, but the dog circled, making pleading, whining noises.

"Go home! Scram! Go away!" Owen said, but the dog wouldn't let him alone.

At the light Owen had to hold the dog down to keep him from running out into traffic. There was no collar, his coat was spattered with dirt, and he seemed to be shivering, although it wasn't that cold.

"Go home!" Owen yelled again, right into his pleading face.

Owen crossed with the green light and the dog sat, looking sad and abandoned, until the light changed. Then, still carrying the rock, he sprinted right in front of an old truck that luckily was slow in starting.

"You can't come to school!" Owen yelled. He walked away and the dog sniffed and whined at his feet once more.

School was very close now. Other children on the sidewalk looked at Owen strangely as he knelt to wipe the slobber off his hands onto the grass, and was licked in the face for his troubles.

"Go home! Now!" Owen yelled.

At last the dog seemed to understand. He trotted back toward the traffic lights.

Owen walked away quickly. But just before the school gates the dog caught up with him again. This time he deposited the rock at Owen's feet, then backed away in shivery anticipation.

Owen picked up the rock and tossed it back along the sidewalk, just missing two girls who were walking, new notebooks and pencil cases pressed to their chests. The dog sprinted by them, chased down the rolling rock, pinned it with his forepaws and then opened his jaws enormously to lift it again in his mouth.

Owen ducked inside the school yard just as the bell rang. The school was as big and dark and forbidding as ever, and he felt the familiar nervousness of the first day. Old as the school was — it looked as if it had been there since the Egyptians — everything on this day was new and up for grabs. Owen followed the long lines of children along the corridors and up the stairs to the classroom to which he had been assigned at the end of the previous year. Outside that room, however, instead of an orderly line, he found a mob of children around the door. A list of names had been posted, including Owen's.

"We have to go to a portable!" Joanne Blexton said.

They all walked back outside to a drab wooden building on the edge of the playground. Though newer, it reminded Owen of his own rickety house. It looked like it had been pulled together out of a couple of garden sheds. The boys and the girls formed up in separate, parallel lines outside the door.

In previous years Owen would usually do his utmost to make sure he was beside Sylvia in any such line. Then he wouldn't look at her, but would be safe in the knowledge that they would be married. But now he didn't care. He just fell in haphazardly, and looked without special interest to see that he would be marrying...

Martha Henbrock, who was half a head taller than him, and who snorted like a horse whenever she laughed!

Suddenly, wet gobbering lips smooched up and down Owen's neck and ear, and he whirled to find the dog up against him again. Owen stepped back and pushed hard to get him off. All the other kids laughed and called out to the dog, who deposited the same muddy rock at Owen's feet.

"What's his name, Owen?" someone called. "Mucus Face? Why did you bring him to school?"

"I didn't!" Owen said. He hurled the rock as far as he could out into the empty playground. The dog took off like a racer, his lean body close to the ground, ears flying back in the wind.

"Children! That's enough!" someone commanded, and Owen and the others turned to face their new teacher.

She was much younger than he had expected, and she seemed very small for a teacher, though she had large, frizzy hair.

The children slowly reformed their lines. The teacher waited until they were silent before addressing them again, this time in a much softer voice.

"My name is Miss Glendon," she said. "And you are the very first class of my teaching career!" A scarlet blush took over her face.

"Oh, brother!" Martha Henbrock muttered.

Owen heard the dog's snuffling, slobbering form getting closer and closer. He closed his eyes and wished himself miles away. But when he opened them he was still in line and the dog was kneeling in front of him, snorting and whining in gleam-eyed excitement over the muddy rock.

"Shh!" Owen said under his breath, and he kicked the rock a few feet away. The dog pounced on it instantly and returned it to Owen's foot.

"Is this your dog?" Miss Glendon asked him. A teacher's brand of broken glass had entered her voice.

"No!" Owen said.

"He seems to know you," Miss Glendon pressed. "Do you have something of his?"

"Just his goobery rock full of dog germs!" Martha Henbrock snorted.

The boys' and girls' lines dissolved, and Owen found himself at the center of everyone's gaze. He quickly picked up the rock again and threw it as far as he could over the roof of the portable. The dog dashed after it immediately.

"We should go in right away!" Owen said, wiping his sticky hand on his trouser leg.

Miss Glendon hesitated a moment, then stood aside and let the children in. Owen, who was at the end of the line, was just able to duck in as the dog rounded the corner of the portable, the rock dripping from his mouth once more.

"Get out of here! Go away!" Owen yelled before shutting the door.

He hung up his jacket and chose a desk near the window. The dog was running around and around the portable now, looking to see where Owen had gone.

Owen hid his face in his hands.

If Sylvia were here this would be funny, he thought. She would pick a seat next to the window so she could watch the dog, and maybe for once in his life he would get to sit beside her.

Instead, at this very moment, she was choosing her seat in a brand-new school far away, in Elgin, where there was no drooling dog, and no Owen.

Owen turned to see, sadly, who was occupying the seat next to him. It was… Martha Henbrock. Without saying a word she passed him a note.

"Get a load of her!" it said.

Miss Glendon was standing in front of them.

"Children!" she said. "Education Board regulations require that I draw your attention to the fire exits." And she pointed to the closet. Already the armpits of her blouse were soaked with dark stains.

"You can smell her, she's so nervous," Martha whispered.

Miss Glendon broke her chalk and misplaced her notes, and sweat formed on her forehead when so many of the children squeaked their chairs against the floor and dropped their pencils one after another.

"I think she's going to cry!!!" Martha Henbrock wrote later in one of her notes. Miss Glendon's eyes were puffy, and she seemed unsure what to do when Dan Ruck's ruler whirled across the room like a boomerang and bounced off the

40

shoulder of Amanda Little, whose notebook spontaneously exploded, with blank pages fluttering everywhere.

And for most of that first hour the dog continued to run around and around the portable, the huge rock still dripping in his mouth. Finally he put down the rock, then sat and whined at it just beneath the window where Owen sat.

At recess time Owen decided to stay in to towel down the blackboard and avoid the dog, and perhaps catch a glimpse of the multiplication code if Miss Glendon had left it out on her desk. She was so inexperienced she might make that mistake on the first day of school, Owen thought.

Miss Glendon was sitting very still, her thin fingers clutching her face.

"I tried to cook my own egg this morning," Owen said.

She didn't move, didn't say anything.

"There were eggs everywhere!" he said. "Every time I turned around I broke another egg!"

She didn't even seem to be breathing. Owen saw text books open and sheets of paper with small, scratchy notes. One page, which he could only see partially, did have a strange collection of numbers. Owen tried to keep them straight in his head. Seventeen and nineteen and twenty-three and a string of others that disappeared under a grammar book.

Did they have something to do with this year's multiplication code?

"Last night I was trying to listen on the crystal radio just in case," he said. "Sometimes there are aliens in the area."

"Are there?" she asked finally in a tight little voice.

"Sometimes. Are you not from around here?" he asked.

"No," she said.

He thought maybe she would explain where she was from, but she clammed up again.

She seemed too young to be a teacher, like someone who suddenly had to be grown up and act like she knew it all when she didn't.

"Sometimes there are aliens," he said. "But we had a fire instead, and I got caught out on the drainpipe. I almost broke my neck. But it was all right in the end."

"Yes?" she said. Owen thought she sounded a little more hopeful.

So he said, "Uncle Lorne was on the radio, so that just goes to show that anything can happen."

"Can it?" Miss Glendon said uncertainly. She had raised her head by then and Owen got a better look at her. Her face did seem quite pretty, behind all that hair, and she had green eyes that glistened, but her lower lip was raw from where she'd been biting it.

There were a few minutes left in recess, so Owen excused himself and ran outside. Other kids were playing with the dog now, throwing his rock for him. A huge crowd had gathered. Kids were yelling and cheering.

Then the principal, Mr. Schneider, came out. He looked like he had aged during the summer, and was now over a hundred. Perhaps he had grown an inch or two as well. He strode into the crowd without saying a word, and all the children fell away.

Owen watched as the dog placed the sodden rock at the principal's feet and then backed up, squirming and begging.

"Whose dog is this?" Mr. Schneider asked darkly.

No one spoke up. Owen had the feeling that if

he opened his mouth the asphalt on the playground might buckle and swallow him whole.

"So, you're nobody's dog," Mr. Schneider said. He bent down slowly and picked up the rock and looked off in the distance, as if trying to find the point farthest from the school to aim for.

"Get away! Get off the property!" Mr. Schneider growled, and the dog backed away. Then Mr. Schneider wound up — his arm was as long as a major leaguer's — and the dog crouched, ready to explode and give chase.

But instead of throwing the rock far into the distance, Mr. Schneider hurled it straight at the dog.

Owen watched in stunned silence. The dog rose to nab it, but somehow managed to turn at the last instant, catching the full impact on his chest and foreleg. He yelped pitifully and hobbled a step or two while the old principal lurched after him.

Some of the older boys laughed and jeered. Then they went after the dog, picking up stones to hurl at him and whacking his back legs with sticks. The bell rang but it didn't seem to matter. The principal went on yelling at the dog, and the boys kept chasing, while the dog ran and hopped with his ears flattened, his foreleg bleeding.

"You leave him! Let him be!" Owen called, but no one paid any attention.

In just a few moments the dog was chased off the school property. Many of the boys would have gone after him if the principal hadn't reminded them that the bell had rung. Recess was now over.

Back in class Owen stared out the window. He didn't know if he wanted to see the dog back again or not. He somehow felt as if it really were his fault that the dog had got into such trouble and was now injured. He couldn't stop wondering how a principal could throw a rock at a dog, a friendly one at that.

On his way home after school Owen saw the dog lying low in the weeds by the side of the road. He had the same rock, but he was shivering, and the wound on his foreleg was black with dried blood. Owen squatted beside him and scratched his ears, smoothed back the silky fur between his eyes and along his strong neck.

"What's your name, boy?" Owen whispered. The dog closed his eyes and licked at his sore leg.

They walked home together. The dog limped

and carried the rock for a time and then dropped it, so Owen picked it up.

When they got to the house Owen gazed at where the upper portion of the drainpipe had been and at the wreck of it now on the ground. It seemed impossibly high, where he had been dangling just the night before.

"You stay here," Owen said, dropping the rock by the steps.

In the kitchen Margaret had put a large bowl and some eggs on the table. Owen cracked them one by one. He got used to the feeling of egg on his fingers, and how much pressure to use in the cracking and the splitting. Many of the first eggs had broken yolks by the time they squirmed into the bowl, but toward the end the new yolks were firm and round and whole. Owen could imagine them sizzling in the pan just like his father's.

"So how was your first day?" Margaret asked him. "Was there anybody new or just the same old crowd?"

"I brought a friend home," Owen said.

"Where is he?" Margaret asked.

"I left him outside."

"Owen!" Margaret said. Owen followed her

down the hall. "When you bring somebody home you don't just —"

She went out the door.

"Oh, no. Owen! No." But then she saw that the dog was shaking, that his leg was hurt.

"Wherever did you find him? What's his name?" she asked.

Owen concentrated on the second and more important question. He didn't say the first name that occurred to him. This dog was a boy and it simply wouldn't do to call him Sylvia.

"Sylvester," he said. "Sylvester the dog."

There were all kinds of things that Owen wanted to say to convince his mother to keep him. But he said the strongest thing he could think of right at the beginning.

"He chose us. I think we *have* to keep him," he said.

"I don't know," Margaret said doubtfully, but she was stroking his bad leg. "Dogs take a lot of work. You have to walk them and feed them and —"

"So are broken eggs," Owen said.

"What?"

"A lot of work," he said.

Owen felt his mother looking at him, as if she

might be wondering, almost for the first time, what sorts of carnivals and circuses might be going on in his mind. They both scratched and stroked Sylvester's ragged fur, and the dog sighed and crooned.

"Broken eggs *are* a lot of work," she said finally, with just enough light in her voice to fill Owen with hope.

THE CODE

"DAD will never let us keep him," Andy said. The three boys were sitting on the front steps soothing Sylvester's black hair with Leonard's brush, which had the softest bristles. The dog trembled and rested in the shade on a bright white bath towel that Owen had found in the guest cupboard along with a matching facecloth that he wet and used to wipe off the last bits of dried blood.

Now Margaret was in the kitchen fixing supper, and the boys were left to greet Horace with the news.

"He might like Sylvester," Owen said hopefully.

"He doesn't like anything these days," Andy said. "It's because of his work."

"What is his work?" Leonard asked.

Andy snorted.

Owen didn't know either and he was glad that Leonard had asked.

"Selling insurance," Andy said. "It means you tell people about all the horrible things that might happen to them, and then they pay you money."

"So the horrible things won't happen?" Leonard asked.

"So when they do happen you'll be protected," Andy said.

"Protected from what?"

"From people asking too many questions!" Andy said, and he glared at Leonard.

Just then Horace's car pulled up, the tires sending gravel sputtering ahead. It was an old car but new to the Skyes, a real station wagon with wood on the doors like a stagecoach in the movies. Horace had bought it for less than a hundred dollars from a friend who owed Horace for a load of lumber that Horace had given him after he'd decided not to build a new front porch.

Owen watched his father get out of the car. His blue jacket was wrinkled from the drive, and he had opened his tie so that it hung loose around his neck like a rope.

As soon as he saw the dog, his face clouded.

"What's this?" he asked. Owen pleaded as hard

as he could silently. But Horace said, "No, no, I'm afraid not. There's no way —"

But Sylvester whimpered and moved his paw pitifully, so Horace knelt down to feel the dog's leg. Owen was amazed at how gentle Horace's fingers became, how intently his eyes narrowed. Sylvester flattened his ears and Horace smoothed them down to the tips until the dog sighed.

"How did this happen?" Horace asked.

Owen told him the whole story. When he got to the part about Principal Schneider hurling the rock at Sylvester from just a few feet away, Horace became nearly as angry as he was the time the boys had flipped Popsicle sticks at cars on the highway and almost caused an accident.

"How could they let somebody like that be in charge of children?" he fumed. "What a disgrace!" And he stormed into the house.

Leonard and Andy followed to see what he was going to do. Owen stayed with Sylvester, but he could hear it all from the steps anyway. There was the angry whirl of Horace dialing the phone, then a pause while Owen held his breath.

"He's not answering!" Horace said finally, his voice shaking the house.

"Dear, calm down!" Margaret said. "I'm sure he's gone home after work."

"He just injured a poor, defenceless dog! What kind of man —"

There was the sound of more dialing, and finally Margaret said, "No, darling, please — "

"I will!" Horace insisted.

"You should calm down!" Margaret said. "You shouldn't be calling him at home."

But it was too late.

"Hello!" Horace yelled into the phone. "Is this Principal Schneider? What kind of jackass do you think you are?"

Owen couldn't believe his ears. He'd never heard his father say that word before.

"You want to know who *I* am?" his father said. "I'm Horace Skye, and I've got three sons in your school." He proceeded to name them all, starting with Owen, so that Principal Schneider could make no mistake about who they were.

Owen gasped in horror.

"That's right!" Horace yelled. "And the dog you injured this afternoon, that was my dog. And I can tell you, sir —"

Instead of telling him, however, Horace fell

quiet for a time. Then he said, "Well, I don't care about…"

But he did care enough to listen a while longer.

"Yes, I understand there are by-laws," he said then, in a more subdued voice. "But I have to tell you that my dog wouldn't — "

He fell quiet again.

"Certainly," he said at last, in such a quiet voice that Owen had trouble hearing. "I can see that opening the school grounds to dogs would pose a safety risk. And you're absolutely right, sir, that you do hold your policy through the company I work for. I'll have to check the fine print, but you could well be correct in saying that allowing animals on the property might undermine your coverage…"

A slight gust of wind came up and Horace's voice became wispy and impossible to follow.

A little while later Horace came back out on the steps and sat beside Owen and Sylvester. He looked like a kite come too hard to ground. He felt up and down Sylvester's leg again.

"Nothing's broken," he said finally. "He'll be fine in a day or two."

"So we can keep him?" Owen asked.

"We'll see," Horace said in a tired voice.

They fed Sylvester scraps of leftover sausages. Margaret wouldn't let the dog share the boys' bed in the attic, so he slept on the steps on an old blanket they found in the garage underneath the rusted remains of an ancient push-mower.

In the morning the leg was still sore. Horace lingered on the steps before going off to work, nuzzling the dog's long nose, scratching up and down his furry body.

"We're going to have to get him a brush and some proper food," Horace said. "And a collar with tags. I can register him in town. If you boys get in any trouble with that principal — "

When he stood up he had dog hair all over his suit.

"I think you've done enough, dear," Margaret said.

Owen was worried that Sylvester might try to follow him to school again, but the dog remained on the steps, licking his leg and guarding his rock.

At school the kids in Owen's class were even wilder than the day before. Miss Glendon was soft and trusting and had trouble seeing several different directions at once. And so spit balls flew like hail while she wrote on the board with her back turned. Owen was struck twice by shots from Dan Ruck, who often was so bored in school that he could barely get his head off his desk. Owen didn't dare fire back in case Miss Glendon caught him and sent him on to Principal Schneider.

Finally Miss Glendon lost her temper and called a snap multiplication quiz. In a quiet fury she handed out blank sheets of paper.

"Just write the answers. I'll give you ten seconds per question. Ready?"

She started firing off questions. Owen gripped his pencil tighter and tighter, and the numbers swam in his mind. What was twelve times six? He thought about seventy two but wasn't sure. What if you now subtracted nine? Then it would be sixty-three. Or if you added four and divided by two it would be thirty-eight. What if you were supposed to switch the digits for even numbers and multiply by three for odd?

He fell two and three and four questions behind, erasing and scratching out and thinking some more.

He wasn't the only one having problems.

Martha Henbrock held her hair in her fist in frustration, and others said, "Wait!" and shot their hands up and held them there with their other hands when they became tired. But that, too, was a mistake.

"No questions during the quiz," Miss Glendon announced. "Only answers!"

Owen scored zero out of forty, the very worst in the class. But almost everyone had done badly. Only Michael Baylor had passed — and he scored thirty-nine, so he must have known the code and not told anyone. It was just like him to keep it all to himself.

Miss Glendon handed back the test sheets in furious silence.

"There's no room in the curriculum for us to review the times tables!" she said. Her voice was strained and the cords of her neck stuck out. "We're going to have a test like this every day!" she said. "What are fractions going to mean when you can't even handle multiplication?"

Exactly! What would they mean? Owen wanted to explain to her that she needed to tell them the code for that year. It might be against some teacher's union rule but it made the most sense to him. If she told them straight out then they'd all do better on the tests and she wouldn't get so upset as a new teacher and look bad.

It was the kind of thing that Leonard might have asked if he had been there. But Owen was frightened. Miss Glendon might think that he was stupid. Or that he was trying to cheat, to get the teacher to just tell them straight out what they were supposed to solve for themselves.

She was on to social studies now. Owen watched her draw a large map of the Pacific Ocean on the blackboard. She had acres of blue chalk for the water and white for the whitecaps and green blobs for the Hawaiian Islands.

Owen couldn't help himself. His hand shot up.

But she didn't turn around. She was engrossed in outlining the coasts of North and South America. Owen's arm turned numb and he felt the hot surge of embarrassment climb his face as others in the class stared at him. Martha Henbrock passed a note to Joanne Blexton and they both looked at Owen and snorted. Dan Ruck was getting ready to fire another spitball.

Then Michael Baylor and two others on the

far side of the room dropped their social studies textbooks at precisely the same time. Miss Glendon whirled and glared at them. She turned to Owen.

"What is it?" she said in a murderous voice.

Perhaps now, he realized suddenly, was not the best time.

"Ask your question, Owen," she pressed.

"I, uh," Owen stammered.

"Don't waste our time!" Miss Glendon snapped. "What is it?"

One more second of confusion and Owen was sure he would be on his way to the dog-hating Mr. Schneider.

"Nothing," Owen said meekly.

"Stand up!" she said.

Owen rose but his knees started to shake.

"It's about math, Miss Glendon," he said.

"Are we doing math now, Owen?" she asked cuttingly. Martha Henbrock snorted again and snickers ran through the room.

Owen said, "No, miss," and his legs folded, letting him miserably back down into his seat. Dan Ruck's spitball hit him on the right eyebrow and he wiped saliva off his face.

"Stand up, Owen," Miss Glendon ordered again. He did as he was told. "I want you to feel free to ask questions in this room," she said. Her eyes looked fierce. "There is no such thing as a stupid question. Now, what did you want to ask?"

Owen cleared his throat. "I was wondering," he said, "if you could give us the code for this year. I think it would help all of us in the quizzes."

"What code?" she asked.

"The multiplication code," he said.

"I beg your pardon?"

Now Owen was stumped. It was hard to imagine how to be any clearer than this.

"The right answers," he said slowly, "for this year. For the times tables," he added.

"Sit down!" she said curtly. "Stop wasting my time!"

"But the answers change!" he blurted. "And you need to tell us or else —"

"Owen, the times tables don't change from year to year."

"Yes, they do," he said quickly. "Every summer the teachers meet and decide what code —"

A great gulping crash of laughter shook the room, drowning out Miss Glendon's puzzled expression and driving Owen back into his seat, his heart pounding.

Had Miss Glendon missed the meeting because she was new? Maybe the other teachers had failed to tell her about the new code?

"The multiplication tables," Miss Glendon said loudly, in an effort to calm down the rest of the students, "are exactly the same this year as last, and always will be the same, now and forever. I promise you, Owen."

The awful truth dawned on him.

Owen walked home after school in a fury. As he approached the house Sylvester ran out joyously to greet him, hardly favoring his bad leg at all. He dropped his rock at Owen's feet and backed up imploringly in his familiar way. But Owen ignored him and slammed the door on his way into the house.

At dinner that evening, Margaret asked Owen if anything was wrong.

"No."

"How was your day at school?" Horace asked. "Everything all right?"

"Fine," Owen said in a tight voice. He didn't want to give Horace something else to laugh about.

"Owen's sad because of Sylvia Tull," Leonard piped up. They were having spaghetti, and three long noodles were sticking out of his mouth. He'd made a volcano of meatballs on his plate and some of the lava sauce was spilling onto the place mat.

"Who's Sylvia Tull?" Horace asked. A note of delight had entered his voice — the same one, Owen recognized, that had been there when he was telling Owen about the multiplication codes.

"She's Owen's girlfriend," Leonard announced.

"What? Do you have a sweetheart?" Margaret asked.

Owen couldn't stand it anymore. He threw his napkin on the table and bolted from the kitchen.

He thought of going to the bedroom, but he knew Andy and Leonard would be up there in minutes, bugging him about Sylvia.

So he ran outside and went around to the old coal chute and slid down into the basement where Uncle Lorne used to sleep. It was dark there but nowhere near as scary as it used to be before Lorne fixed it up. In the old days the Bog Man would sometimes leave the nearby fields and slide and gurgle in the slimy, cobwebbed shadows of that basement.

But now it was a refuge. Owen found Uncle Lorne's cot in the gloom and he lay there staring at the ceiling beams. He heard his brothers roaring around the house looking for him. It was only a matter of time before they rooted him out, but for now it was good to be alone, to be still.

It hardly lasted a moment. Owen heard snuffling and whining noises, and there in the gloom beside him was Sylvester. He had brought his slimy rock, and he laid it gently on Owen's stomach. Then he licked his neck and started circling, circling on the floor beside the cot before finally flumping into place.

Owen's family continued to call for him. He lay as still as possible and stared at the ceiling, dull in its shadows, and yearned for an adventure. Something — a tidal wave, maybe — to get him past the puddle of his problems.

THE CONSOLATION OF
THE LOON

ANDY had a new theory about the immense, dark shadows that appeared now and again under the surface of the slow-moving, brown-watered river that flowed at the bottom of the hill near the Skyes' old farmhouse. For a long time the boys had thought the shadow was caused by a giant squid that hid in the mud, its tentacles swaying in time with the murky reeds on the riverbed. But a new book in the library shed light on a different possibility.

"I think it must be a plesiosaur!" Andy announced, and he showed the picture of the enormous beast to Owen while Leonard looked over their shoulders. It was late Friday afternoon and school was finished for the week. Two entire days stretched before them crying to be filled.

The picture showed a long-necked sea monster with jagged teeth snapping a large fish in half. Most of the body was lost in shadows beneath the surface, exactly the way the shadows on the river disappeared into murk.

"We could use the boat," Andy said. It was an old abandoned pirate fighter they'd noticed weeks ago on the shore of the river just past Mr. Michael's pig farm. It did float, but one of the seats had broken when Andy stepped on it too hard, and the oars were different lengths.

"It will be fine if we stay close to shore," Owen said.

The three of them went down to the basement to sort through the complicated and extremely valuable gear that Uncle Lorne had left behind when he moved out to marry Lorraine. There was a heavy metal box full of monster lures, some of which had barbed hooks the size of dog teeth. The boys also found a small but springy rod with steel line that they could use to drag the beast close to the boat. There was also a sturdy net that, if they lashed a broken hockey stick to the shaft, they could use to reach high into the air to trap the giant's head.

Horace saw them dragging their gear upstairs.

"What a great idea!" he said. "Why don't we all go fishing!"

Margaret called them for dinner then and they took their seats around the table.

"I know just the lake," Horace continued. "I haven't been there for years. Lorne and I used to go. It's got the most beautiful clear water — "

"But —" Andy said.

"Why don't you give Lorne a call?" Margaret said brightly. "You could take all the children."

The boys sat in shock.

"Not Eleanor and Sadie!" Andy managed to say.

"Why not?" Horace asked. Andy started to explain about the plesiosaur in the river, about the true nature of their planned expedition, but Horace wouldn't hear of it.

"You want a real adventure?" he said. "You come camping with me."

"Besides," Margaret said cheerily, "you need to get to know your cousins better."

A gloom settled over the boys' dinner. Andy stared hard at his fork, and Leonard rested his head on his hand so close to his plate that it looked like his face might slump into the tuna casserole. Owen felt his food stick in his throat like wet sawdust.

"What is your problem with Eleanor and Sadie?" Margaret asked finally. "They're lovely girls."

"Sadie has woggly eyes," Leonard said miserably.

"No, she doesn't."

"She does when she looks at me!"

"And Eleanor is... Eleanor!" Andy said. His neck went stiff simply speaking her name.

"We'll all have a great time!" Horace said, like a judge sentencing them to hard labor. There was no point arguing anymore when he said things that way.

"Yes, absolutely. You will all love it," Margaret said.

Owen listened to the strained sounds of family cutlery sawing through the silence.

At last Horace said to Margaret, "*You're* coming, too, of course?" There was much less finality in his voice than just a few minutes before.

"I can't leave Lorraine all alone," Margaret said, and her eyes were large and innocent, with hardly a woggle in them.

That night, just before sleep, Andy said, "Maybe the lake we're going to is a landlocked glacial depository."

"A what?" Leonard asked.

"A trap," Andy said, "for plesiosaurs. That's what happened at Loch Ness. The monster was caught there. If we get up early and get the boat, we could bring it with us to the lake."

Owen's eyes got heavier and heavier. He had a dream of Sylvia sitting in the prow of the old boat, keeping watch. She had the net between her knees and her hand kept trailing in the water. Then the water turned dark, and the boat began to rise. Owen tried to tell her to move her hand away because the monster's jaws were getting closer. But the right words wouldn't come. Finally he stood up and the boat started to rock and she screamed at him.

"Come on! Let's go!" It was Andy, shaking him awake.

Owen rubbed his eyes and opened them, then shut them again and fought to get the dream back. There might still be time to save her!

But she was gone in the mist.

Leonard, still asleep, was making snuffling doggy noises with his mouth until Sylvester, who was now allowed to sleep inside, licked his face. Leonard struck out at the air and said, "Down, Sadie, no!"

But finally he was awake, and the three boys snuck out of the house in the cold early light with Sylvester sniffing the ground ahead of them. His trusty rock was in his mouth all the way.

"How are we going to get the boat back to the house?" Leonard asked.

"It's not that far," Andy said lightly. "We'll just carry it."

"But it's uphill most of the way!" Leonard said. "And that boat weighs more than we do. I think we should bring the cart."

"The cart! The cart!" Andy hooted. "How is the cart going to hold up something as heavy as the boat?"

"A lot better than I will!" Leonard replied, and he went into the garage and got it. The cart had been a Christmas present to all of them years before. It had a solid plywood construction and four tough steel and hard rubber wheels.

"It better not slow us down," Andy muttered.

They ran like warriors up to the main road and then down the hill and through the woods and across the railroad tracks, the cold breeze smarting their faces. The cart bounced wildly behind Leonard as he pulled on its frayed rope.

At the river the old boat listed in the weeds at the shore. It was even more sunken and tired than Owen had remembered from the last time they'd seen it. Large patches of crackly green paint had fallen off, and there were dents on the side of the massive craft. Somehow rocks had ended up in the water in the bottom of the boat, and the bow now sported a hole the size of a boot where the wood was crumbling.

The boys inspected the damage. Luckily the hole was high enough that it wouldn't be much of a problem.

Under Andy's orders, Owen and Leonard reached into the boat and cleared the rocks. Then they all heaved mightily until the boat was wrestled out of the weeds. They hoisted it on its side — it seemed as large as a beached whale — until most of the water had drained out. Then they strained and pulled again. But they could only move it a few more yards before the boat settled as if made of concrete.

"I told you it was too heavy," Leonard said.

"Don't be such a weakling!" Andy shot back.

"Let's use the cart," Leonard suggested.

"We'd just break it!" Andy insisted. "Come on! You're not trying hard enough."

In response Leonard walked over to the edge of the water and started scanning the horizon with his hand shading his eyes.

"You two keep lifting," he said. "I'll be on the lookout for plesiosaurs."

Surprisingly, the boat seemed a bit lighter without Leonard's help. Straining and pushing, the boys managed to move it more than a dozen paces up the trail before collapsing in exhaustion.

"It's no good," Owen said. "It's too waterlogged. We'll never get it to the house like this."

"We could use the cart!" Leonard called.

"All right," Andy said wearily. Leonard's face brightened and he pulled the cart beside the huge boat.

But then the shadows changed and Sylvester barked, and Owen looked back up the trail.

"It's Eleanor and Sadie!" Andy groaned. "What else could go wrong?"

Eleanor called out to them. "We've been sent here at the crack of dawn to find out what pathetic activity you're up to now." Sylvester ran to her and deposited his rock at her feet, then began circling her and whimpering.

"It's not pathetic," Andy said. "We're going to haul this boat up to the house so that we can launch it to find and capture a long-lost plesiosaur who's been hiding in the depths of the lake for millions of years!"

Sadie made woggly eyes at Leonard, who looked red-faced at the ground.

"Pathetic," Eleanor said. "Don't you know that plesiosaurs are extinct? Not to mention the fact that a boat that big will never fit on a little cart like that. The axles will buckle."

"This little cart has held far more than this boat in its time!" Andy said. "It's had huge boulders and airplane parts, and anti-submarine missiles…"

"And a collection of robot heads," Owen called.

"And enough mud to build the pyramids!" Leonard yelled.

"Pathetic," Eleanor said again. She picked up Sylvester's rock then and held it suspiciously between two fingers.

"What am I supposed to do with this?" she asked.

"Just throw it," Andy growled.

So Eleanor wound up and threw it as far as she could out into the river.

Sylvester ran to the water's edge and yelped and barked helplessly. He took a few steps into the water, then backed up and barked again and pleaded with them all.

"What did you do that for?" Owen cried.

"What?" Eleanor said. "It's only a dumb rock." She bent down and picked up another one. "Here, boy," she said, showing it to Sylvester. "Chase this one." She threw it a little way up the trail. Sylvester sniffed at it briefly, then returned to the water's edge whining and whimpering.

"That's Sylvester's special rock!" Owen said. "It's the only one he loves. He won't go for any other."

"Oh, come on!" Eleanor said. She picked up a different one and called out, but Sylvester didn't even look at her.

Andy took off his shoes and socks and rolled up his trousers. He tried wading into the water, but it was too cold.

"We can't even go out and get it for him!" Andy said bitterly. "Look what you've done!"

"So he's in love with a dumb rock," Eleanor said. "Tell him to get over it." She took Sadie's arm and turned away. "We were instructed to tell you to report back home in five minutes or else the camping trip is off," she said. "Apparently fish only bite in the early morning when most of us should be sleeping."

She pulled Sadie along with her.

"Bye, Leonard," Sadie said.

"That's it. That's it!" Andy said angrily. He pulled on his shoes and socks, then ordered Leonard back to his post at the side of the boat. He wrestled the cart into place and took the side opposite Leonard, commanding Owen to the stern. Together they lifted. The weight shifted toward Leonard but Andy strained and the boat came crashing down on top of the little cart. But the axles held.

The cart looked like a midget lifting a whale.

"It's working," Leonard said. "It's my idea and it's working!"

They struggled and sweated and puffed and roared, and the huge boat slowly rolled up the trail.

Sylvester remained at the shore, whining and whimpering for his lost rock.

"Come on, Sylvester!" Andy called. "We have to go!" And they all yelled for the dog.

Sylvester seemed torn between joining the boys and staying by the last sighting of his rock. He barked and yelped pitifully. Finally he plunged into the water and began swimming frantically around, biting at the waves.

The boat started to roll back down the trail.

"Keep pushing!" Andy said raggedly. "We'll come back for Sylvester when we get the boat to the house."

"But there won't be time!" Owen pleaded.

"We have no choice!" Andy argued.

They huffed and strained. Slowly the boat rolled up the trail through the woods and over the railroad tracks. Under the tremendous load the wheels of the little cart dug into the dirt and every bump threatened to topple the load. But once they reached pavement the cart rolled much better, and at the crest of the hill it became even easier.

Owen looked down the slope of the driveway in the distance where everyone was standing near the car: Horace and Margaret and Lorne and Lorraine and the two girls. A huge pile of luggage littered the lawn. The car trunk was open and Horace stood with his hands on his hips staring at the bedrolls and backpacks, the loose blankets and pillows, the tents, sleeping bags, axes, shovels, ceramic mugs, plates and bowls and many other things waiting to be packed.

The boat began to roll on its own toward the house. It was fun not to have to push, but to just jog beside the craft and keep hold. Leonard yelled out and waved, and Horace and the others turned their heads to see them coming. The girls were looking, too, and so Andy picked up the pace.

"Eleanor said we could never do it!" he said.

Then Sylvester joined them. He was soaking from the river and shivering like a fool, but he ran right up to Owen and seemed almost to fly with joy.

"What have you got there?" Owen said. And he had to look twice before he blurted, "It's his rock! Sylvester must have swum underwater to get his rock!"

Sylvester dropped the rock right at Andy's feet, so Andy had to stop then and pick it up.

"It *is* his rock!" Andy said. "Look at the shape of it!"

Owen examined it intently. There was no mistaking —

"Hey! *Help!*" Leonard called. Owen looked up and saw the boat screaming along like a runaway train. Sprinting flat out, poor Leonard could barely keep up and wasn't strong enough to slow it.

It was heading straight for Horace's car.

"Look out!" Owen called, and he and Andy started running, but they were too far behind.

The others scattered in all directions just as the runaway hit the side of the family car.

It was hard to say which was tougher. The car hardly moved, but sustained a prow-shaped dent in the wood of the passenger door, while the boat jumped back and fell off the cart, but was otherwise undamaged.

One car window on the side unhit by the boat fell out and left a gaping hole.

Owen and Andy stopped some distance from the scene. Horace was glaring at them across the driveway with laser heat in his eyes. His fists were doubled and he wasn't moving at all. He wasn't even inspecting the damage.

"I don't think we're going camping," Andy said in a little voice.

It was a long day. The boys cleaned up the luggage and put away all the equipment. They dragged the boat behind the garage and stored the cart again. Then they raked the lawn and tidied up the basement and scrubbed the dirt from the floor in their room and tidied even the corners of the closet. There was hardly anything to say in their gloom.

"It's all Eleanor's fault!" Andy muttered. "If she hadn't thrown Sylvester's rock in the river, none of this would have happened!"

But Owen found himself thinking about Sylvia. It seemed more and more as if everything in his life was going wrong since she'd moved away.

In the evening, unexpectedly, Uncle Lorne showed up to make the boys a campfire. He said he felt badly about cancelling the trip. The girls had stayed behind with their mother, but Leonard was too tired to go down and Andy claimed he wanted to stay in the bedroom and plot a proper revenge against Eleanor. Horace sat inside and read the newspaper in such a bad mood that no one wanted to disturb him.

Lorne made the fire in the backyard away from

the apple tree and the house, close to a stone wall where the first farmhouse had been built on the property long ago. It was a dark, chilly night. Owen pretended he could hear the lap of the water against the shore of the lake, but actually it was cars on the highway in the distance. Margaret stayed just long enough to warm her toes. Then she went inside.

Owen and Lorne were alone with the stars and the fire. Lorne was as tall and thin and bony as ever, and his hands were scarred and marked from working with boilers for so many years.

"It's been an awful day," Owen said. His eyelids drooped with fatigue. Sylvester was exhausted, too, but he at least had his special rock, which was tucked under his chin as he lay by the fire. Owen told Lorne about the miraculous recovery and Lorne nodded.

"I used to know an underwater dog," he said. "He caught a fish once and came up all splashy and proud. But he got these spines stuck in the roof of his mouth. Turned mean after that."

Lorne faded into silence. He was a man of few words in general. Owen had been dying to ask him about being on the radio, about the bird songs, but he didn't feel he could, somehow. Silence wrapped around Lorne like a blanket you didn't feel right disturbing.

Owen was trying so hard not to bring up the subject that he started whistling on his own without really thinking about it. He scrunched his lips into a small hole and curled his tongue and blew, letting loose a short, hard shriek. Lorne immediately turned and looked at him.

"Use your throat, too," he said, and he let out a haunting loon warble, his cheeks flapping like loose sails. The sound split into three or four echoes. Then it rose in a single note that broke halfway up and swirled into different parts again before dying out over the road like a lonely trail of fireworks.

Owen tried again and felt jiggly in the throat.

"You have to be wild," Lorne said. "Let yourself go." Lorne closed his eyes then, and the sound that came out was black cold water and darkest night that turned into a ripple of notes punctuated by huffing and loneliness, by hard sighs.

Owen tried again with his eyes closed. The first few sounds were ugly, but he surprised him-

self after a moment when a strange trilling vibrat-
ed through his body.

"That's it!" Lorne said. "That's a start." And he
trilled, too, both below and above Owen's voice at
the same time. When Owen's breath gave out,
Lorne seemed to be doing three trills at once, till
Owen came back in again.

And for a time it didn't matter about the lost
camping trip. They were two loons, one small and
one large, who might have been singing at the side
of a cold lake in fall. When they were finished,
Owen felt like he had a long neck and fished
under water and cried out regularly in the dark for
a single mate lost somewhere in the wild.

POLITICS

ANDY was obsessed with the idea of getting back at Eleanor. For a while he wanted to lure the girls into the basement and have the Bog Man come and threaten to suck out their brains through their eye sockets. But the Bog Man had been unreliable lately and as quiet as a ghost, and the basement was nowhere near as scary as it used to be.

Then Andy was sure the girls would be terrified of aliens arriving, and for a time he tried to revive the crystal radio. But it didn't work nearly as well after the fire in their bedroom, and the boys had no other way of contacting distant galaxies.

It was a difficult problem, this issue of revenge.

For Owen, schoolwork was much easier now that the mystery of the multiplication code had been put aside. Twelve times six stayed put and eight times seven never moved and four threes were content the way they had always been. He found he had a lot of spare thinking time to try to keep his memory of Sylvia alive. He gazed out the classroom window imagining her moving toward him in her orange coat, her small form getting larger and larger. He tried to see the softness of her skin and the bright dance of her eyes. But the harder he looked, the blurrier she seemed to get. She was like a sandcastle in his brain, crumbling at the edges in the wind and water.

Miss Glendon became more comfortable in front of the class. She had a way of becoming still now and looking at the author of any disruption much like a snake will look at a little mouse trapped against a tree root. And slowly, fewer spitballs flew through the classroom air space. Rulers stayed rooted more often, and the dark wet patches in the underarms of Miss Glendon's blouse became smaller.

She got her hair cut one day and suddenly looked very pretty. Her face had more shape and her eyes seemed larger. Gradually, before Owen knew what was happening, the Sylvia in his mind began to look more and more like Miss Glendon.

Once he realized that Sylvia was changing this way, he tried hard to stop it. When he mentally walked her around the schoolyard she remained herself perfectly as long as she kept her distance and didn't turn around. But when she got close, she was Miss Glendon in Sylvia's clothes.

He was losing her.

Before she moved away he had given her a ring that made her invisible to everyone else. Now she was becoming invisible to him and turning into someone else in his mind.

Owen stayed in for recess one day, cleaning the blackboards and chatting with Miss Glendon the way he did from time to time. The weather had turned cold and the sky looked gray and full of unfallen snow.

"Sometimes I wish things didn't have to change so much," Owen said, just to make conversation.

"Do they?" Miss Glendon said. She seemed to be only half listening. She was marking an arithmetic test about which Owen was unconcerned.

"If you think about it, nothing stays the same even one day to the next."

"Was everything so good before?" she asked.

She looked at him now, her red pencil poised in mid-air.

"No, it wasn't all so good," Owen said. "But when I thought about how it was going to be, it was going to be better than it is now."

Miss Glendon glanced at Owen in a curious way. For a moment it seemed like she had gazed deep into his thoughts and knew everything — how she was replacing Sylvia on those long walks in his mind, how her scent lingered in the air whenever she walked along the aisle past Owen's desk.

Her words surprised him completely.

"We're going to need a class president," she said. "You should think about it."

"Class president?"

"Yes. I'm going to introduce the idea this afternoon. I'd like the class to join the Junior Achievers program, and to do that we need an executive body — a president, vice-president, a secretary and a treasurer. I think the other children really respect you, Owen."

Class president! Owen felt himself swell with the words. It was hard to breathe, his chest suddenly felt so presidential.

"What do you think, Owen?" she asked.

"All right," he said after a moment.

All afternoon his heart beat like a military drum while he waited for the announcement that he, Owen Skye, had been named president of the class. The title ran through his mind in an endless song. President Owen. Excuse me, Mr. President. Owen Skye, Class President! In his own mind he heard his name pronounced so often, and in such admiring tones, that he was slow to respond when Miss Glendon actually said it out loud. Martha Henbrock had to punch him on the shoulder, and then he stood up expectantly, as if acknowledging applause.

"Well?" Miss Glendon said, a look of great inquiry on her face.

"Thank you. I accept," he replied. Everyone laughed, which made Owen feel quite gratified, and he turned to look at his friends, his supporters.

"Owen," Miss Glendon said. "I am asking you what is the capital of Belgium?"

"Of Belgium?" he replied. For a moment he was in complete confusion. He imagined that she was asking him, as the new class president, to represent them all in Belgium for some important reason.

"Yes. Of Belgium," she said.

Owen's jaw slowly lowered in a puzzled and non-presidential way as he realized that he was simply being quizzed. No appointments had been made, and his fellow students in fact were laughing directly at him and not with him over the issue of Belgium.

The pressure to say something, anything, grew enormous.

"Boston," he blurted finally, and wished at once that he had remained in noble silence.

"Sit down, Owen," Miss Glendon snapped. "Pay attention!"

Owen felt his spirits sink. Why had Miss Glendon dangled the prospect of the presidency in front of him and then snatched it away by embarrassing him in front of everyone? For clearly she had changed her mind about him. The class president would know the capital of Belgium without even thinking. Such facts would be in his blood, would be part of his presidential nature.

Miss Glendon wouldn't even look at him now. Her eyes were everywhere except on him. She was obviously casting around for other candidates who knew their basic geography.

When she finally brought up the topic of the Junior Achievers Club near the end of the day, Owen sat in misery, hardly following her words. The hands on the clock on the wall above her head stopped moving, as if they'd been glued in place.

Then Martha Henbrock punched him in the shoulder again.

"Owen?" Miss Glendon said. Apparently she had just asked him another question.

Owen stood up.

"Brussels," he said, his jaw clenched. Everyone laughed again.

"You have been nominated for president, Owen. Will you accept to let the nomination stand?"

The floor seemed to be falling beneath Owen's feet.

"Yes," he said weakly, and he sat down again.

Once more drums began beating inside his chest, and he had to breathe through his mouth to get enough air. He had just become president. Yet again, how quickly life changed. There would be important decisions to make, although what they might be he couldn't say.

Had there ever been a president in the Skye family? Possibly not. Not even Andy had been president before.

He focused on the board again, forced himself to pay attention despite the enormity of his new status. He saw that under the word *President* there were four names, and his was not even at the top of the list. It was fourth, behind Michael Baylor, Martha Henbrock and even that lowly spitballer Dan Ruck.

Why would Miss Glendon list four presidents? he wondered.

Then he listened more carefully.

"Candidates," Miss Glendon said, "please prepare your speeches for Monday. Then we will vote and form the executive. Are there any questions?"

Owen felt weak with questions. Wasn't he already president? Why did he have to make a speech? How long should it be? What should he talk about? What did the president do, anyway?

The bell rang and Owen sat still and befuddled, and when he walked home it was in a non-presidential way, with his eyes on the ground and no drums beating to mark his steps.

At the kitchen table Owen poked his finger into a glass of milk and tried to salvage part of a cookie that had fallen in. He explained everything to Margaret, as much as he understood.

Finally she said, "So you've been *nominated* for class president."

"But there are others nominated, too!" Owen said.

"Yes. The class will have to choose," Margaret said, as if it were perfectly reasonable to start off with four maybe-presidents and then disappoint three of them. "You'll have to think about what you want to say in your speech."

At the dinner table Horace took up the topic.

"School is so limiting," he said as he carved the meatloaf. "I read in the newspaper the other day about one class going all the way to Japan. The teacher had started them off by linking up pen-pals, and after some months a lot of the kids were really good friends, and they did a few bake sales. And the school principal was related to an airline pilot. The next thing they knew they had cheap tickets. So they all went to Japan and had the time of their lives. School doesn't have to be so boring. There's plenty of time to be bored once you start working."

"You should go to Gibraltar," Leonard said.

"What do you know about Gibraltar?" Andy challenged.

"It's on the same latitude as Japan," Leonard said. "If Owen could go to Japan, then he could go to Gibraltar, too."

"Maybe we should think of what's possible," Margaret said.

"But Japan is possible!" Horace argued. "The newspaper was full of that class that actually went there."

Owen chewed his meatloaf in a worried way. It felt as if his presidency was running away from him.

"What did that class do in Japan?" he asked.

"They went to temples. They learned Japanese!" Horace said. "I forget the details."

The whole family worked on the campaign over the weekend. Andy found important information about Japan, such as the fact that Samurai warriors were able to slice through armored bodies with a single stroke of their swords, and that airplanes flying to Japan might have to crash land in the Pacific Ocean if there was ice on the wings.

Leonard made a big banner that read *School Doesn't Have to Be So Boring* in black and red Japanese-style lettering.

Margaret worried over Owen's election suit. His jacket and pants that had been fine just a few months earlier had tightened hopelessly. But Andy's suit would do as long as Owen rolled up the cuffs and wore two sweaters underneath and a strong belt.

"I don't think I need to wear a tie," Owen said, frowning in front of the mirror. It was going to be hot in the two sweaters, and he hated the scratchiness of a collar snug around his neck.

"Of course you have to wear a tie," Horace said. "Little things make the difference. How are you going to raise thousands of dollars to get to Japan if you aren't even willing to wear a tie?"

Owen wrote out his speech on foolscap sheets. Then, following Andy's direction, he transferred it onto Margaret's recipe cards using the tiniest printing he could manage and eliminating the spaces between words. In the end Owen's hand ached but he had managed to get every word of the speech onto four little cards. Each card now looked like an inky, meaningless congestion of letters.

"But I can't read it!" Owen said in despair.

"You aren't supposed to," Andy said. His eyes looked full of extra years of learning. "All this printing helps you memorize it."

Owen practiced his speech in front of the mirror.

"Some people are content to confine their education to little portable classrooms," he said. "Others have shown us that Japan has classrooms, too, and we could go to school there for a time, and eat rice, and if there was an earthquake we wouldn't have to read about it in the newspaper because we'd be right there for once." He tried to look serious and confident, like the man who read the television news.

At school on Monday morning nobody else was wearing a suit. Michael Baylor had on an argyle sweater with a stiff-collared shirt, but no tie, and Dan Ruck was in an old brown sweatshirt that smelled like it might have been used to towel down horses, and Martha Henbrock was in a gray dress she'd worn many times before. Her shoes, however, were shiny black patent leather with silver buckles.

Owen's dress shoes didn't fit so he had just slipped on his classroom shoes, a pair of desert boots handed down by Andy months before. Both laces had been snapped and re-tied with tiny knots, such that it now took great skill to tighten the laces without breaking them again.

Owen sat at his desk and tried to conjure up Sylvia. It took a great deal of concentration now to summon her, to make her eyes blue enough, to keep her face from turning into Miss Glendon's. He thought of how they had walked together to the river and she had told him how her father had hurt his back playing tiddlywinks. He thought he could hear her voice in his head telling the story again, but realized with a start that it was Miss Glendon's.

"Martha Henbrock," she was saying, and the class was applauding, and Martha walked slowly to the front.

She too had tiny cards that she gripped against her belly like a life preserver.

"Miss Glendon, fellow classmates and candidates, thank you for this opportunity to share my views," she said, pronouncing each word painfully, as if moving her jaw through too much toffee. "Every year, children die of terrible diseases all over the world. I think that we, as fellow children, should dedicate ourselves to wiping out disease, malnutrition, poverty and ignorance everywhere. As president of the Junior Achievers, I would spare no effort to aid in the fight for planetary improvement. Even though we are young, we are the future. And without us, there would be none!" She threw her arms out dramatically but dropped her cue cards, which scattered like petals around her feet.

Nobody clapped, until she finally bent down to pick up her cards, and then Miss Glendon began to applaud and others followed.

Dan Ruck was next. He had no cards and he stuck his hands in his pockets and shifted from leg to leg as if standing on board a rocking boat.

"I, uh, well, hmmm," he said, then horked up some phlegm suddenly and looked around, at a loss. Finally he just swallowed it and pushed a hand through his hair nervously. After the hand came down, some of the hair relaxed in front of his eyes, where it had been previously, and some stayed sticking straight up.

The words rushed out of his mouth. "I thought it might be a good idea to have a dance," he said. He blew out loudly, twice, in an effort to catch his breath. "With, uh… just fuddle music. I mean *fiddle!* If you want to make me president," he said in conclusion, "my pa and uncles are fiddlers. That's all."

He bolted back to his chair, and once again Miss Glendon led an uncertain round of applause. Owen found himself gripping his desk in mounting terror.

Next Michael Baylor walked to the front of the class. He was tall and graceful and held his little cards as if keeping them for someone else who might need them.

"Some people," he said, looking out at the class and pausing, the thought apparently just occurring to him, "never get beyond our little world in this small part of the country. We," he said, putting his hands on his hips now and looking down, shaking his head sadly, "might even be among them. Where will we go in our lives? What will we do with ourselves when we get older?"

He looked straight at Owen for a moment until Owen squirmed, thinking he might be expected to answer.

"Children in other schools are taking advantage of these years," Michael Baylor said, "to see the world as their parents have never dared see it. I'm not sure if anyone here read in the newspaper last week about the class that traveled all the way to Japan?"

Something lodged in Owen's throat then and he started coughing horribly and gasping for breath.

"Why couldn't we organize something like that?" Michael Baylor asked. "Aren't we good enough to go to Japan?"

Owen gasped and struggled in his seat. Martha Henbrock whacked his back with the palm of her hand but he continued to hack and wheeze.

"Owen, do you need to get some water?" Miss Glendon asked.

Owen nodded his head in panic and fled the classroom. He bolted across the playground and into the main school, then down the hall and thrust his face into a drinking fountain. He drank and drank and tried to think what to do.

Michael Baylor was saying everything he meant to say!

Some minutes later Martha Henbrock came to get him at the water fountain. "Michael is going to win," she said. "He told everyone his father could bring them to Japan like that other class."

Owen followed her back outside. The wind had picked up just in the last while, and suddenly the first snow of the winter was being driven against the windows and walls of the tired old school and the shivering little portable.

Once inside again, Owen brushed the snow off his hair and his jacket. He walked to the front of the classroom, then spent as much time as he could taping Leonard's banner to the blackboard. Some people tittered. He was hoping that during the delay a massive fire would break out and burn down the school.

His mind felt frozen. He turned to look at everyone. At the back, Dan Ruck sat with his face buried on the desk under his arms. Michael Baylor was beaming and confident, the picture of a future president.

Owen took out his cards and looked at them. The words seemed even more welded together.

He cleared his throat finally and began to speak without knowing what words might come out.

"Michael Baylor," Owen said, "wants us all to go to Japan." He paused, then opened his mouth again. "Japan!" he said, and looked out at everyone — at Martha Henbrock and Joanne Blexton and Miss Glendon, who was standing at the back. *"Japan!"* he said again, and some people began to chuckle. Owen took a step and found that he felt more comfortable, so he started pacing back and forth at the front of the room. "Why not Gibraltar?" he asked, and some more people laughed. "Why not Brussels or Boston or Kalamazoo? Why shouldn't we go to Peru or Mesopotamia or the lost city of Atlantis? If we can go to Japan, we can go to — " And he paused, trying to think of some other place.

Someone called out from the back, "Italy!"

Someone else said, "Ethiopia!" and there were calls for Ireland and Brooklyn and Labrador before Miss Glendon shushed them down.

"This is Owen's speech," she said, glaring at Owen, who at once felt awful.

"Maybe we can go to Japan," he said. "It might be a good idea. But maybe we should start with something easier. It would take a lot of money to go to Japan, and we don't even have pen-pals yet. We don't even know if they would like us. But we could go... to Elgin," he said.

"What would we do in *Elgin*?" Michael Baylor called out, and some people laughed. He looked upset, and Miss Glendon didn't tell him to be quiet.

What would they do in Elgin? Owen looked at the world map on the wall, as if it might tell him. He looked at the clock and the door to the cloak room and at Miss Glendon, who still seemed angry with him. Then he glanced at Miss Glendon's desk, where her papers were laid out, and her pens were standing up in a large metal cup, and her pencils were in another wooden one. People began to get restless in their seats.

"In Elgin," he said, his mind racing. And then he said it again, "In Elgin!" and reached across to the wooden cup and took out the pencils.

He showed the empty cup to everyone. Then he took a penny from his pocket and flipped it high in the air and caught it in the cup.

"We could organize a tiddlywinks tourna-ment... to wipe out world hunger!"

Everybody was laughing now, as if it were all a big joke. Owen tried hard to think of what else he could say to salvage the situation, but nothing occurred to him. He sat down to a roar of laughter and applause. He could feel the blood pulsing in both his temples. What had possessed him to go on like that about tiddlywinks and world hunger?

Miss Glendon handed out ballots and Owen wrote his own name under the president slot in pencil, then erased it and inked in Michael Baylor. Michael looked more like a president and made better speeches and who knew? Maybe his father could buy them all tickets to Japan. What better idea had Owen come up with?

Tiddlywinks.

Miss Glendon collected the ballots, and during recess Michael Baylor shoved Owen in the dirt and said what a rotten jerk he was for making everyone laugh at his ideas. Then when he was on the ground Martha Henbrock told him he shouldn't make fun of world hunger.

Owen didn't fight back. He just felt terrible.

They returned to class to face the results. Beside Martha Henbrock's name was written 7, and Dan Ruck had 0. Michael Baylor had 10. His name was circled and he had become president.

President Michael Baylor.

Owen's name had 9 beside it.

Owen had a hard time believing the result. He would have won if he had only voted for himself. But he was glad that he hadn't. He pulled off his tie and Andy's jacket and one of his sweaters and felt immensely better.

What a relief that he wouldn't have to be president after all!

"Congratulations to all the contestants!" Miss Glendon said. "Michael, I think you will want to convene a meeting of your executive very shortly, since you have such grand plans. Owen, you ranked in second place and so become vice-president. Martha, you are the secretary and Dan, you are the treasurer."

Owen looked across at the gloating expression on Michael Baylor's face and felt a sudden squeezing on his chest. He would have to take orders from Michael Baylor! No wonder they called it being *vice*-president, he thought — this awful feeling of being caught in someone else's grip.

AVALANCHE

MICHAEL Baylor's fingers would not stay still. They tapped against the desk top, the pencil case, the sheet of paper on which he had written notes about the trip to Japan. Owen watched him from the adjacent, vice-presidential seat.

The executive of the Junior Achievers Club was meeting for the fifth time. It was only a week until Christmas and the four elected members had to stay after school and report to Miss Glendon.

"Have we finished the pen-pal letters?" Miss Glendon asked.

"Completed!" Michael Baylor said.

"But have we found a class in Japan willing to exchange with us?" Miss Glendon pressed.

"My father is looking after that," Michael Baylor said.

"Could you please remind him that it takes at

least three weeks for letters to get to Japan. We don't have a lot of time to set up contacts."

"My father knows many people at the municipal and county levels," Michael Baylor said. "And in the business community as well."

"I know, you have explained this, Michael. But do any of them have anything to do with Japan?" Miss Glendon pressed.

"All of them do!" Michael Baylor said indignantly. His fingers kept tapping, tapping.

"What about the airline tickets?" Miss Glendon asked. "Your father was going to approach different companies and service clubs for donations."

"He's still working on that," Michael Baylor said.

"But could you tell us which ones he has approached? Perhaps we could ask some others."

"He *said* he was still working on it!" Michael Baylor snapped.

It grew very quiet around the table. Martha Henbrock was writing notes for the minutes. Dan Ruck had his head on his arms. Owen focused on watching Michael Baylor's fingers.

"Maybe," Owen said, "while we're getting

ready for Japan, we could still plan a little Christmas party."

"What would we do — play tiddlywinks?" Michael Baylor jeered.

"If you like," Owen said in a little voice.

"Well, I was elected to get us to Japan!" Michael Baylor said loudly. "I don't think we have time to waste on little Christmas parties. We need to organize the passports and figure out what gifts to give our hosts. We need to find someone to teach us Japanese!"

There was a bitter silence as Owen regretted having voted for Michael Baylor instead of himself.

"I just thought that Dan could ask his father and uncles to come next week with their fiddles and —"

"Do we want to go to Japan or not?" Michael Baylor asked. "Because I'm doing all this work organizing. I think the class voted for Japan, not fiddle music!"

Miss Glendon told Michael Baylor to watch his tone, and Michael Baylor glared at her.

"I'm doing all this work," he muttered.

Owen walked home in a gloom. It had been

snowing since the middle of November, and now great drifts had blown up against the little farm-house. One side of the house was protected by the apple tree and farther off an even taller, ancient oak, but the other side was exposed. The winds blew snow clear across the fields and piled it against the thin, wooden wall of the house. Three times already the boys had had to shovel the drift down so that the kitchen window wasn't blocked. Even the old boat, abandoned behind the garage, was buried.

As soon as Owen got home Margaret told him, "Don't take off your coat. You need to go outside and throw Sylvester's rock for him. He's been whining all day!" She sounded like she was ready to strangle someone.

Sylvester jumped and howled at the door until they got outside. Owen took the rock around to the back, out of the wind, and threw it into a deep snowbank. Sylvester flung himself into the snow and began digging desperately, howling and whimpering. Then he rose in triumph. He trotted back, left the rock at Owen's feet and began whining and worrying again until Owen launched it even farther into the snow.

He knew Sylvester could keep this up for hours, never tiring, never losing interest in the rock. Owen waited and threw the rock, waited and threw it, wishing that life could be as simple for him. Dozens or hundreds of throws, it didn't matter. Sylvester always came back with the rock in his mouth, desperate to continue.

But even out of the wind Owen was beginning to get cold. His cheeks smarted and his hands felt like frozen meat. He picked up the rock and faked a throw to the left. Sylvester started running but knew in a moment that he'd been fooled. Then Owen faked right and while Sylvester was turned around he hurled the rock right over the apple tree and past the property fence into a snowy pasture.

Sylvester missed it completely. He sniffed Owen's hand and then backed up pleadingly, waiting for the throw.

"It's over there! It's gone!" Owen said, pointing the way. "You go find it!"

But Sylvester wouldn't leave him. He trembled and slobbered and barked and sat back barely containing himself, waiting for the throw.

So Owen had to mount the fence and hoist

Sylvester over. The drool from the dog's tongue froze on Owen's jacket. Together they searched in the pasture for the rock.

It should have been right there. There should have been a hole in the snow where it had fallen. But soon the entire area was full of Owen's and Sylvester's tracks, and various holes where Owen had plunged his arm groping for the rock.

It was gone.

Owen and Sylvester searched the same area over and over. Then Owen branched out and looked past where he could have possibly thrown the rock — unless he'd been seized by a sudden strength. It was hard to say.

The daylight faded quickly and Margaret called him for dinner. Sylvester raced back and forth, sniffing the ground like a hound dog, then almost crawling up to Owen, pleading with him to stop hiding the rock.

"I haven't got it!" Owen cried. "You found it when it was underwater! This should be a lot easier!" he yelled, and he kicked snow in Sylvester's face in frustration.

"Owen Skye! You come in for dinner now!" Margaret yelled.

Sylvester would have stayed out by himself if Owen hadn't dragged him in by the collar.

"What's wrong with the dog?" Horace asked at the table. Owen knew from his father's voice that it had been another bad day at work. Now Sylvester was sniffing and worrying up and down the dining-room as if his rock might be there.

"I lost his rock," Owen said in a little voice.

"Well, you'll just have to find him another one," Margaret said lightly. She was serving up boiled Brussels sprouts that smelled like wet laundry.

"That's his special rock!" Andy blurted. "How could you lose it?"

"Nonsense," Margaret said. "There are a million more just like it. Find another one and he'll never know the difference." She served up the mashed potatoes, too — they looked gray and old, like somebody's grandfather — and one small, tough square of liver on every plate. Owen's smelled like a wet baseball mitt.

"It's the only thing he loves," Owen said sadly.

Sylvester was sniffing under the table now, and Horace lost his temper.

"Owen, put him in the basement if he can't behave!" he ordered.

So Owen dragged Sylvester into the basement and shut the door. Sylvester immediately began to scratch at the wood and whine even louder.

"Let's try to have a civilized dinner," Horace said. That meant no one spoke as they chewed through the tired food, and Sylvester's scratching and whimpering sounded like it was being broadcast over a loudspeaker.

After dinner all the boys went out with Sylvester and swept the field where Owen had thrown the rock. Horace even let them use the large kitchen flashlight reserved only for the gravest emergencies. They joined arms and walked slowly up and down the pasture, kicking deep in the snow.

It was a cold, windy night that offered up a few different rocks, but not the special one, not Sylvester's. The boys stayed out till their cheeks were sore and red and the entire field had been kicked and pawed over and examined in light and darkness. Finally Margaret ordered them in before they perished of the cold.

Sylvester was inconsolable. He whined and muttered at the front door, pleading with them to not give up the search. Owen lay awake deep into the night, thinking not only of Sylvester but of his own Sylvia, how easily she, too, had been lost when he had been least suspecting it.

In the cold darkness, when the house was still except for the creaking of the walls against the winter wind, Owen crept out of bed and pulled on his robe and slippers and walked downstairs in the dark. Sylvester was at his side immediately, wanting to look for the rock some more. Owen was afraid he might wake the others with his whining.

"In the morning," Owen said, and he rubbed at Sylvester's face and ears the way the dog liked it. "Just hang on until then."

Some days before, Owen had made a Christmas card in class for Sylvia. It had little winter sparkles glued in the shape of a snowman. But he had not written anything inside it yet. Owen got it now and sat in the living-room with one small light on and the card on his lap. Sylvester waited impatiently by his feet.

Owen thought of writing, "How is Elgin? Well, Merry Christmas!"

He almost wrote, "I miss your orange coat." And he thought a great deal about asking, "Do you still have the ring that I gave you? I know it's too big but I'm hoping it will fit some day."

It was awful trying to decide on the right words. Finally something occurred to him which he wrote swiftly. He penned *Love* with only the slightest tremble, and signed his name with a flourish. Then he inserted the card and sealed the envelope.

He stared at the blankness of it.

What was her address? He knew his own, and wrote it quickly in the top left corner. And he wrote Sylvia Tull in the middle and wondered at how such a little thing, writing someone's name, could almost conjure her into the room.

But he didn't know where she lived. Elgin, of course, but what street and what number?

Horace had a drawer full of maps in the little room that he kept as his office beside the kitchen. Owen went there now and turned on another little light.

His father stored his important papers in that office along with his typewriter and adding machine, which he used when he brought his work home. That room was full of the mystery of selling insurance. Now that Owen was vice president he knew what it was like to go to long meetings and try to convince people of whatever it was they ought to be convinced about. Horace's office had a smell to it of old suits and something else that Owen was only now beginning to recognize — anxious letter-writing.

Owen pulled open the map drawer. The boys had gotten in trouble before for fooling with those maps. Horace used them in his work when he was meeting new clients and he hated it when the creases tore or peanut-butter stains showed up in formerly clean residential districts.

The map of Elgin was near the bottom. Owen took it out carefully and unfolded it on top of the typewriter. In the past the boys had jabbed its keys and rung its bell until Horace had yelled at them to get their grimy hands off his machine.

Owen had never looked closely at a city map before. He wasn't even sure what he was looking for — just some clue to where Sylvia's house was. But as he looked at the little streets on the map — mere lines, with the occasional school marked, the post office, the water tower — he saw no helpful little note saying *Sylvia Tull lives with her parents here. The house has a swimming pool and boys who want to send her a Christmas card should use the following address.*

Owen's eyes wandered and he noticed on a shelf near the desk the big black binder where Horace kept his client list. It held pages and pages of names and addresses. Owen opened it and flipped through: Campbells, and Dunstans, and Everleighs and Gullsteads. He climbed the alphabet and got to the Tilleys, Todds, Toddlemeyers, Trundalls… Tulls.

Tulls!

Owen held his breath and looked at the page. *Mr. Lee Tull* it said in thick, official type. *Mrs. Elizabeth Tull.* An address was scratched out, and another was written on top in pencil: *1837* was clear, and ELGIN in big letters, underlined twice. The street name was *River*-something — Riverbend? Riverside? Riverworth?

Owen couldn't make out his father's handwriting.

At the bottom of the page it said *Dependant/daughter: Sylvia.*

Owen felt sweat beading on his forehead. Sylvia's parents were clients of his father! Horace had written Sylvia's *name* in his black binder!

Owen was feverish. Even in the muted light, the colors in the office seemed suddenly brighter, even dizzying.

His father had met Sylvia's parents.

His father might even have met Sylvia!

Owen carefully put away the binder and the map of Elgin, and he turned out the little office light. The house was cold but he felt hot at the same time. He returned to the living-room and wrote *1837 Riverbendsworth, ELGIN* on the envelope. He was sloppy on the second half of the street name so the post office would know that he meant whatever the right word was for Sylvia's street.

Still no sounds from upstairs. But Sylvester knew something was happening. He pawed and whined at the front door and soon everyone would be up. So Owen threw on his winter clothes over his pajamas and ran out through the snow with Sylvester and down the road to the spot where the dark highway met the equally black and lonely railroad tracks. Then he plopped the card into the mail box.

The deed was done.

He returned to the house but could not enter

without searching with Sylvester through the field once more. Owen was certain that his luck had changed now that he had written to Sylvia. They kicked and sniffed and looked with renewed faith but found no special rock there.

"In the morning!" Owen promised him. He managed to get himself and the dog in the house and up those loud and creaky stairs and back to bed between his brothers without anyone knowing.

But in the morning Owen could hardly be awakened. He trudged downstairs on feet as heavy as porridge. Sylvester was still whining, still anxious to go out to look for his rock.

"I have to eat breakfast first!" Owen said and walked into the kitchen, which was blinding. All the windows were pouring in white light.

"Sure is snowing out there," Horace said as he tended the bacon.

"The field!" Owen cried and raced to the window. Past the apple tree, a thick new covering of snow had erased all signs of search and effort in the field, returned it to an unspoiled and unmarked state.

"Looks like Sylvester's going to have to find himself another rock," Horace said.

Days passed. Owen and the others looked again in the field but the rock was irretrievable now. Owen began to question not only which field he had thrown the rock in, but whether he had thrown it at all, or if Sylvester had dropped it somewhere. And he began to question whether he had sent Sylvia a card. That whole night seemed like a dream now.

Every morning his mother trudged out to the letter box at the end of the driveway and returned with a handful of colorful envelopes, all addressed to Mr. Horace Skye or Mrs. Horace Skye, who was Margaret, or the two of them. There were snowy trees and glittery snowmen much nicer than the one Owen had made, and sleighs and stars and Santa Clauses with reindeer and elves. And warm-looking houses brightly lit under fluffy snow that wasn't like the cold, heavy, bitter stuff that Owen had searched through looking for Sylvester's one source of joy in life. Cards came from down the street and across the country and over the ocean.

But there was nothing from Sylvia.

Poor Sylvester moped about the house, always wanting to be outside, searching. He could go by himself for hours, sniffing and mumbling, worrying over and over the same ground, and then later racing to some other spot where he had convinced himself the rock might be. For a time he seemed to think it was under the apple tree. Later he switched to burrowing under the snow-shrouded old boat. It was pitiful for Owen to watch the hope sailing in him, to see and feel how he trembled at home when another day was done and his rock had not been found.

The day before Christmas Margaret brought in the mail and handed Owen a card. Owen stared at it in disbelief, then ran upstairs and locked himself in the bathroom. There were marks all over the front of the envelope. He tried to be careful ripping it open.

The card that fell out was blank, though the envelope was filled with sparkles that drifted onto his clothes.

He opened it up and read the little note, in very familiar handwriting: *Dear Sylvia, I am Vice-President now. But you can still call me Owen.*

Why had she sent him back the same card he had sent her? Just because the glue for the sparkles had given up?

He looked again at the envelope. In blurry, black, official print on the front it said: RETURN TO SENDER. INSUFFICIENT POSTAGE.

He'd forgotten all about the stamp!

Disappointment buried him like an avalanche, and Owen felt himself shrinking, shrinking almost to nothing under this mounting snow and mud of daily defeats and bitter failures.

CHRISTMAS

IT was shocking to Owen how the return of that one small envelope could nearly ruin something as momentous as Christmas. In the morning Andy and Leonard roared out of bed in a fever of excitement. Santa had visited in the night. He had eaten the cookies left out for him on a small plate in the kitchen, finished most of a mug of hot chocolate and, surprisingly, had even left part of a glass of Scotch as well. The boys' stockings were now stuffed with packages that, when unwrapped, turned into balsa-wood gliders and scale model fighter jets and plastic robots and watery half-globe worlds that snowed drunkenly when shaken. There was also, as usual, an orange filling the toe of each stocking.

Andy's balsa glider sailed the length of the house and curled back and disappeared into the kitchen. Owen turned his gaze to the presents under the tree. How glorious they appeared in their wrappings, even in the dark shadows before dawn. That tree looked like it could shelter everything a person could want. Owen just wished that among the many bright cards propped in the branches along with the ornaments was one to him from Sylvia.

Even Sylvester was sniffing at the packages as if his long-lost rock might be there.

"Let's make breakfast," Andy said. "So Dad won't have any excuses."

Last year at Christmas Horace, who was awake by six-thirty most mornings of his life, could not be roused until almost nine o'clock. Then he insisted that no presents under the tree could be opened until breakfast had been served and eaten and the dishes cleaned and put away. So now Andy started the bacon and Leonard managed the toast, and when they were ready Owen expertly cracked six eggs into the big pan and cooked them gently. He even managed to flip one of them without breaking it. Andy squeezed the stocking oranges and Owen filled the sink with hot soapy water so that the dishes could be done the instant people stopped chewing.

They were in luck. The coffee percolator still

had grounds in it from the day before, so Andy set it on the stove and when it started to boil he poured out two stiff smelly mugs' worth. Then the boys sat back and looked at the clock.

It was three minutes past six.

"Leonard, go see if they're awake," Andy ordered.

"Why me?" Leonard asked, using his whining voice that cut through the chilly morning air like freezing rain.

"You don't have to wake them up," Andy said firmly. "Just open their door and see."

"We could take them their breakfast," Owen said.

Their parents couldn't possibly be upset at that. Leonard knew where the trays were and the boys loaded them up with cutlery and napkins and all the food they had prepared. Then they carried the trays to their parents' door.

It seemed deathly silent.

"Open it!" Andy urged. He and Owen held the trays. Leonard was the only one with a free hand.

"Maybe we should wait," Leonard said.

"What for?" Andy replied. "If Dad was asleep we'd hear him."

That was true, Owen thought. The whole house knew when Horace was asleep.

Andy kicked off a slipper and reached up with his bare toes to turn the knob. Just for a second Owen glimpsed their parents, large lumps in the gloomy room, completely still and huddled together under the blankets. Then Sylvester bounded through the door and started sniffing and whining under the bed.

"Breakfast is served!" Andy announced and pushed his way into the room. Leonard switched on the overhead light.

Horace snapped upright and looked around as if under attack. His face was a horrible shade of gray, his whiskers the beginnings of barbed wire. Margaret raised her head, too, and looked at them with unfocused eyes.

"What's going on?" Horace demanded.

The boys froze.

"Get out of here!" Horace barked. "Turn the light out!"

Andy turned so quickly that the orange juice on his tray spilled onto the egg on Owen's. Then Owen tripped over Leonard, and in a moment coffee was soaking into the wallpaper, and the one unbroken egg, which Owen had saved for his mother, was being lapped up by the dog along with all the bits of jam and butter that had not yet been ground into the rug.

"Blast you!" Horace roared, and when he twisted into action the covers slumped off the bed and onto a puddle of spilled coffee.

It was almost eleven o'clock before they got to the presents under the tree.

Lorne and Lorraine and Eleanor and Sadie came over in the middle of the afternoon. By then the presents sat in odd piles in different parts of the house: socks and sweaters and mittens and books, and complicated board games with a thousand tiny pieces. Together the boys had worked for weeks to build their parents a crossbow that launched small sticks the length of a room. But the one demonstration shot that Andy fired caromed off a sofa cushion and hit Leonard in the glasses. The crossbow was banished to the basement immediately, and when the girls arrived all the children were ordered outdoors as a matter of sanity.

"Now's our chance!" Andy gloated as the boys pulled on their winter gear. The girls were already outside, shivering in the wind. "Finally we can pay Eleanor back for throwing Sylvester's rock in the river!" All the disasters of the day seemed to roll off him in anticipation of what was to come.

"How are we going to do that?" Leonard asked.

"They've never been to the haunted house," Andy said. "Let's take them now and leave them there. They'll be scared out of their brains and we'll have to rescue them!"

"Why would we want to rescue them?" Leonard asked.

"Because that's what you do with girls," Andy said.

"Just the girls you're in love with!" Leonard said.

Andy blew wet air into Leonard's eyes. It wasn't quite spit, but Owen was close enough to tell it wasn't completely dry, either. Leonard's face filled with outrage just as Margaret said, "What's going on here? Why are your cousins freezing outside while you three dawdle in here?" Then she opened the door and pushed them all out into the cold.

"What are we supposed to do now?" Eleanor

asked. She and Sadie were shivering in a dull patch of sunshine in the small shelter of the south wall of the house. Sylvester raced around begging them to go to the field to look once more for his long-lost rock. He jumped up and pressed his paws against Sadie's shoulders, knocking her back, and licked at Eleanor's face even as she shoved him away.

"Dog slobber! On Christmas Day!" Eleanor said in a disgusted tone. She wiped her face with a hankie that she pulled from the sleeve of her coat. "Is this the afternoon's entertainment?"

"I know a place," Andy said calmly. "If you girls are brave enough. Probably you aren't."

"You go ahead," Eleanor said.

"Aren't you even curious?" Andy stammered.

"Knowing you guys," Eleanor said, "it's probably filthy, or freezing, or really dangerous, or completely boring, or all of the above."

She looked right back at Andy until he turned away in disbelief.

"So I guess you don't want to meet the Bog Man's wife," Andy said finally. "You don't want to go to a real haunted house and be scared out of your wits and learn something for a change."

"Why would I want to meet the Bog Man's wife?" Eleanor asked.

"She's very interesting actually," Leonard said. "She's had a really tragic life. I met her once on Halloween."

"You did not," Eleanor said firmly. "But if you three go, we'll watch you make fools of yourself. If Leonard walks with Sadie," she added.

Andy jabbed Leonard through his snow jacket and silenced the protest that was trying to emerge.

"It's a deal!" he said.

Quickly Andy started them on the way to the woods. It was so cold the wind made them weave back and forth on the road as if they were avoiding enemy fire. But at least it was a relief to enter the shelter of the trees.

But the trail had filled in with weeks and weeks of snow. Even Andy floundered to his knees. Eleanor and Sadie were unhappy in their Christmas dresses. Poor Leonard had to walk beside Sadie and pull her out of the worst of it and brush the snow off her legs. Sylvester fought his way gamely, as if swimming. He struggled in front of them and behind and around and between all the nearby trees, as ever sniffing and whining for his lost rock.

"It's not very far!" Andy said. "You'll be able to climb the rafters and try out the red couch that the Bog Man brought up for his wife to sit on while she was dying."

Owen knew that Andy was giving just enough details of the story for Eleanor to ask for more. But she stayed quiet.

Owen scanned the woods for signs of the house. They'd never gone in the winter before. Everything looked different. The fir trees were weighed down with heavy loads of snow, the old trail was invisible, and it was impossible to tell where they were.

"When we get there," Andy whispered back to Owen, "we'll boost them in through the window and then leave them for a while. I can't wait to hear Eleanor screaming for help."

But when Eleanor spoke finally, it wasn't to scream.

"You're lost!" she said. She had stopped walking and stood with her arms folded across her chest. "Where is this supposed haunted house anyway?"

"It's very close," Andy said, and he looked at her in exasperation. "Keep going. You can't just give up!"

"Why not?"

"Because people who give up never get to Mars or the South Pole or the bottom of the ocean."

Owen watched the two of them. Eleanor and Andy were nearly the same height, but at the moment Andy looked smaller. And usually when he gave a command to his younger brothers they did it. But not Eleanor.

"I think we should go home," Eleanor said.

"Just a little farther!" Andy pleaded. It didn't sound like his voice at all. He turned to go on and Owen followed, but he wasn't sure anyone else was coming. Finally he sneaked a look behind him. Some distance away, but walking in the right direction at least, Sadie was clutched onto Leonard's arm while Eleanor trudged grimly behind.

They walked and walked. Owen kept his eyes peeled. He was hoping that something, anything, would begin to look familiar. These were the woods they could ride their bikes through at top speed at night in the summer and never lose their way. They knew at all times exactly where the river was, where the train tracks crossed, how far to the highway. But the woods seemed much deeper now, and today was Christmas so there was no noise. The river was frozen, the trains weren't running, the road was deserted. It all might as well have been a hundred miles away.

Then Sadie fell into a drift up to her neck and almost disappeared. She crawled out kicking and sputtering with snow in her eyes and boots and down the collar of her coat.

"I don't care how haunted the house is," she declared. "I'm going home!"

She stomped off crying, and Eleanor went with her while the three boys watched, uncertain what to do.

"Well, that's torn it!" Andy said finally and ran off after them. He was right, of course. It would be awful to have the girls return to tell Margaret they'd been abandoned in the woods by their cousins on Christmas day.

Leonard followed Andy and so did Owen. Now Eleanor was leading the way but at least they had their old tracks to stay in.

"I can't believe it!" Andy muttered. "Our one big chance and we can't even find the haunted house!"

"Maybe we shouldn't be scaring people on Christmas," Leonard said.

"It was a gift!" Andy muttered. "And we've wasted it."

They walked and they walked. They walked so far that the trail began to get firmer, as if people had been treading on it for weeks. Already the light was beginning to fade and the air felt colder with every passing minute.

"You've gotten us lost!" Andy announced at last, with the first glimmer of joy in his voice.

"I'm just following your big fat tracks home again," Eleanor responded.

"Yes!" Andy exulted. "That's all you had to do, follow my tracks. But we've been going around and around. Don't you see?" He pointed at the snow, where there were traffic jams of footprints, some going one direction, others going the opposite. "This is at least the third time we've passed over this ground," he said with undisguised satisfaction.

"I can't help it if your trail was flawed in the

first place," Eleanor said. "You were so lost you crossed over your own tracks, too."

"I did not!"

They argued about it as darkness descended. Owen felt the chill of the forest reach inside his jacket and pull the heat from the center of his bones. The trees looked like dark skeletons standing silent watch.

But not that silent. Owen was suddenly aware of the creaking of timbers, of the awful tension surrounding them, as if the whole land was holding its breath.

"Let's just get home!" Owen said.

"That's fine, but which way is it?" Eleanor countered.

"Help!" Sadie screamed suddenly, in a voice so piercing that Leonard tripped over a fallen branch hiding behind him in the snow. He floundered for a moment and finally stood sneezing with snow up his nose.

"Let's be calm," Andy said in his old voice again, the steady one that relished these sorts of predicaments. "Let's think our way out."

"It's almost dinner time," Eleanor said, squinting at her watch. "Which means that Lorne and your father are going to be coming for us any moment." She started screaming as well. "We're over here! Help! Hello!"

Andy took two strides across to her and fit a mitted hand over her mouth.

"Don't be ridiculous!" he said. "We're only lost. What glory would there be in having someone come and get us?"

She pushed his mitt off her face. "Glory?" she said. "Who cares about that?"

But she didn't scream again. So everyone looked at Andy.

"You have to think your way out," he repeated. "That's the most glorious way." He thought for another moment. "Captain Volatile never screams for help." And he puffed out his chest and looked as if he might leap over the trees any moment to impress her.

"Our lives are in danger and all you can think about is comic books!" Eleanor muttered.

They all stood silently. Owen tried to open his eyes as wide as possible to take in what little light there was. The snow helped. It didn't really seem so dark after all. The trees emerged from the shadows and took form. He could see everyone's breath in vapor clouds that rose and disappeared above their faces. Even Sylvester stayed quiet for a time. And there seemed a heaviness to everything, like the snow weighing down all these limbs, and the way sound was muffled in the forest, swallowed by the cold air and the sad carpet of winter.

And then, slowly, surprisingly, the outline of the haunted house made itself known to him.

They were standing quite close, in fact. Suddenly it seemed so obvious that it was hard to imagine they had missed it. Owen looked at the faces of the others, but they didn't see it, even though they were looking straight at the tired, snow-draped frame, the crumbling walls and vacant windows.

"There it is," he said quietly and pointed exactly where they were all looking. Then, as if he were conjuring it, they saw it for themselves.

"It was right here all the time," Andy said.

"Is that it?" Eleanor said. "Is that what we've been walking all day to see? I froze my face for this crummy little wreck of a house that's more trees than anything else?"

"It doesn't matter," Andy said in disgust. "You

wouldn't appreciate it anyway. Let's go home. At least now we know the way."

"No, we came this far," Eleanor said stubbornly. "Let's see what's so special about this stupid place." And she marched off the trampled trail and waded through the hip-deep snow.

The old house looked desolate and lonely to Owen, as if time had been leaning heavily on it. Part of the roof at one end had fallen in, and trees that Owen hadn't noticed before were now growing out of several of the windows. It didn't look safe to enter.

"The door's locked," Andy called out to Eleanor. They were all following now. "You have to go through the window."

Eleanor put her hand on the doorknob anyway and pushed hard. The door opened and she stepped inside.

"Watch out for the hole in the floor!" Andy yelled, running after her into the house.

"I don't want to go!" Sadie said suddenly.

"It's all right," Leonard said, and he took her arm. "She's very nice — for a ghost."

Inside, the light was eerie. Everything was covered in snow and shadows. Eleanor and Andy had both managed to walk around the hole in the floor. Owen and Leonard and Sadie walked around it, too, and approached the red couch, which was where it always was, in the middle of the room. Eleanor and Andy were sitting on it now, quite close together, as if drawn there magnetically. It, too, was full of snow. Owen dusted off a section and sat down carefully, and then all five of them were on it. Owen gazed up at the snowbound forest through the rafters above his head.

He looked around to see where the Bog Man's wife might be. Maybe in the winter the house got so cold and lonely that she went somewhere else.

Owen heard a low whistling in the trees and a rubbing of branches against something.

A voice came then, soft as falling snow. It was hard to make out. Owen had been shivering but now he felt like he was sitting beside a fire. He couldn't follow the words exactly. They sounded normal and yet not usual at all, as if spoken in a foreign language or a dream.

There was the voice, and the silence of the air sifting through the forest — which was in itself a sound, Owen realized. And the sound of snow being quiet, and of the haunted house bearing the slow weight of time. The more he listened, the more he heard — a slight scratching, a tree perhaps giving in, finally, to a dreadful itch, and then the sudden staccato of something, maybe a mad woodpecker knocking after frozen insects. And he heard his own breath sliding in and out, a little furnace of heat and activity in the midst of all this cold and stillness.

Owen let go his loon call then. It started low and soft and warbly, and slowly took over his throat and chest and shook the flimsy walls of the haunted house until it felt like loose snow was being shivered free. The others stayed where they were and just listened.

Later they walked home together in silence. Andy was apparently not interested anymore in scaring Eleanor and Sadie, and Eleanor said nothing about the house being boring or ordinary or somehow not worth the hours of cold marching.

At Christmas dinner Horace muttered over how the little paper skirts Margaret had made for the turkey legs were interfering with his carving, and Leonard spilled cranberry sauce on the pure white tablecloth. The silver of the cutlery shone in the candlelight and turkey gravy pooled in the mashed potatoes and buttered squash, and little bits of cork floated in the adults' wine glasses. Uncle Lorne drank three glassfuls and agreed to whistle for them all. He filled the house for a time with so many birds that Owen felt like he might have been back in the woods. Margaret wore a red dress that Owen had never seen before, and she kept her apron on during dinner. She never seemed to settle in her seat, but was constantly moving back and forth between the dining-room and the kitchen.

So many things were the same as every other Christmas, and yet so much was new as well. Even after everyone else was finished, Owen's plate remained nearly full. Not because he wasn't hungry, but because he was so busy just looking at all that was new and old. They had never had Eleanor and Sadie and Lorraine for Christmas before, yet now it seemed perfectly natural that they would be there. Lorraine seemed so happy, even though she was fatter than Owen had ever seen her. She wore a purple velvet dress that might as well have been a bed sheet, it was so floppy.

"I remember when Eleanor was a baby,"

Lorraine said, helping herself to more mashed potatoes. "She wouldn't sit still for anyone, and at Christmas dinner I had to march up and down the hallway singing nursery rhymes while all my guests served themselves."

Owen looked from the belly of Lorraine to Eleanor's blushing face, from the face to the belly, and the belly to the face. It was just like looking at the snow on the trees until the trees had turned into the haunted house. Right before his eyes Lorraine and her fat belly turned into something else.

Something else indeed.

Finally Owen began to laugh. The more he looked, the funnier it got, until he was sobbing up against Leonard and clutching to keep his head above the table.

"What's so funny?" Margaret asked, but Owen couldn't say it. His eyes were full of tears.

He writhed and wriggled at people's feet like some animal possessed by a giddy fever. And the more he fought, the harder it was to gain control. His body became a shuddering mass of gasping laughter. Leonard, too, succumbed, and Sadie, and it spread through the room until Owen wondered if the table would be overturned.

"Whh..hh..at are we… l.ll..llaughing about?" Margaret sputtered, but Owen couldn't trust himself to speak. Lorne had collapsed on the sofa and Andy and Eleanor were puddled together by the television set and even Lorraine was clutching herself and leaning against the doorframe as if she might fall over.

"It's…it's…nothing," Owen said finally. And through the teary slits of his eyes he watched his aunt Lorraine holding herself — herself and her secret baby — and felt as if the whole world was jiggling in their joy.

CALENDARS

MICHAEL Baylor came back from Christmas holidays looking nervous. At a Junior Achievers meeting in front of the class he announced that everyone had to sell calendars to raise money for the trip to Japan. The calendars came from Michael Baylor's father's company and showed different classic tractors from years gone by. January featured a delicate 1940 John Deere Model H painted green and yellow. A girl in a straw hat and clothing unsuitable for farm work sat on the metal driver's seat trying to look comfortable. February was a 1929 McCormick-Deering perched like a bull on a hill, the front wheels spread wide and dark body silhouetted in the sun. March was a yellow 1939 Farmall A with bright red wheels.

Michael Baylor said that if they sold the calendars for five dollars each, then only four dollars would go to his father to cover his costs and that would leave one dollar per calendar for Japan. "If we all pledge to sell a hundred calendars," Michael Baylor said, "then we would raise two thousand six hundred dollars for the trip." He also said that his father was president of the Good Neighbors Club, and they would donate fifty cents for every dollar raised on the calendar sale. He made a quick calculation and then announced a final fundraising figure that seemed so large, Owen thought they would be able to go around the world several times on it.

The class was silent for a while. Finally Dan Ruck said he didn't even *know* a hundred people.

"You don't have to know them to sell them calendars!" Michael Baylor said. "Just go door to door. It won't be hard. These calendars will sell themselves. In fact, you don't need to limit the sale to one per household. These are collectors' items and some people will want to buy several."

Miss Glendon said she wanted to get on with her lesson. "Why don't you call a vote, Michael, to see if people agree to sell these calendars?"

"We *have* to sell them," Michael Baylor said, "if we want to get to Japan!" He looked around the room like he was daring anyone to vote against the calendars.

The vote was called. No one put up a hand except Michael Baylor. Owen fingered the sample calendar nervously. *Beauties of the Ages* it said on the cover.

Owen raised his hand.

Soon others raised theirs, and then almost everyone was voting to sell the calendars.

Each student took a hundred home in a box. Owen hid his in the bedroom closet and tried to work up the courage to ask his father for help in selling them. But that evening he found Horace sitting in his favorite chair, his face hidden behind the newspaper. Owen could tell from the snapping sound of the turning pages that his father had had a bad day.

So Owen waited until Friday when Horace was usually in a better mood. When Horace got home late in the afternoon he threw his tie on the chesterfield and ruffed up Sylvester's fur in a happy way. Then when he was reading the paper he joked about an article about a chicken with two heads and no feet. "Sure would have trouble crossing the road!" he said. Then he looked at Owen.

"How was your day?" he asked. "You look like the prison bars are closing in all around."

Owen screwed up his courage.

"I was wondering," he said, "if you could drive me into Elgin."

"What for?"

"I have to sell calendars. It's to go to Japan on the class trip," Owen said.

"I thought you lost that election," Horace replied. His voice was suddenly sharp as wire, and Owen wished he hadn't brought it up.

"Yes, but — "

"Show me these calendars."

Owen brought the box down from the bedroom and opened it for his father.

"Tractor calendars!" he said with that special note of delight that Owen knew to dread. "You'd be lucky to sell two of these. You'll just be wasting your time."

Owen went to Margaret to ask if she would drive him into Elgin. But Horace followed him into the kitchen.

"You'd do better if you sold the *tractors* door-to-door!" he said.

"What's all this about?" Margaret asked.

"His class thinks they're going to Japan!" Horace said sharply.

"Didn't you plant some idea like that in Owen's head?" Margaret asked.

"But he wasn't even elected," Horace said.

It was strange for Owen to see his father whirling like this, saying something one day and then the opposite another.

"These are just young kids!" Horace said. "How do they think they're ever going to get to Japan?" Horace looked at Margaret straight over Owen's head. "Do you know what he wants? He wants me to drive him all the way to Elgin. After I've been working all day! Do you know I've been to Elgin twice already this week? People in Elgin don't buy anything! I can tell you that for a fact. And these ridiculous calendars…"

Owen retreated to the bedroom and closed the door. He felt like he was caught so tight under a giant's foot that he could hardly breathe.

Before dinner his mother took him aside. "You know that your father has to sell things every day," Margaret said. "It's a difficult life and some days don't go right. He didn't mean what he said." Owen could hardly look up at her. "I called

Lorne," she said finally. "He'll take you to Elgin."

Lorne arrived in the truck after dinner. Owen snuck out the back with his box of calendars so that Horace wouldn't ask him where he was going.

On the dark ride to Elgin, Owen tried not to think of what he would say if he happened, by chance, to knock on Sylvia's door.

He thought about explaining to Sylvia that he had written her a Christmas card but had forgotten the stamp. He still had the remnants of the card, without sparkles, in a drawer underneath his socks, and wondered now if he should have brought it with him to present to her in person. Better late than never.

"Where do you want to start?" Lorne asked him when they got to Elgin.

"I don't know," Owen said.

They drove down the main street. The gears groaned and the truck had a bad habit of veering into the wrong lane when Lorne looked too hard at the buildings and signs. Then he would turn the wheel violently in correction, and Owen had to hug the door to keep from getting an elbow in the face.

He peered in the darkness to try to see the

street names. He saw Lansdowne and Sellwig and Tuttle and Ramsworth, but nothing that started with a River.

Lorne let him off on Bunton Avenue. Owen didn't carry the whole box with him, just a few calendars. He walked up one long, snowy lane and mounted the front steps. The house looked old and dark, like a trap.

Owen pressed the ringer and stood back. He turned around to make sure that Lorne was still sitting in the truck in case he had to make a run for it. Who knew what kind of murderer was living behind that door?

But there was no answer. The house was deep in gloom and silence. Owen rang the bell again, just to be sure, and then a third time because he was pretty certain now that no one was home.

Just as Owen turned away, the door opened and a woman older than dust hissed at him, "What do you want?"

She was hunched almost double, with one shoulder knotted to just below her ear. Her hands looked like gnarly tree roots wrapped around a cane.

Owen stared at her in a panic.

"Well?" she spat.

"I need to go to Japan!" Owen blurted, and he waved a calendar at her.

She looked at him with hatred. "Catch my death because of you," she said, then disappeared behind the gloomy door.

Owen ran back down the lane and vaulted into Lorne's truck.

"Let's try another street!" he said urgently.

Lorne drove him to one called Maple Grove. The houses looked friendlier and had snowmen in the front and scatterings of Christmas lights, even though Christmas was over. Owen decided to try the house with several hockey sticks stuck in the snowbank lining the driveway. He rang the bell and lifted himself on tiptoe to peer into a round window on the door. Instantly a light went on in the hallway and he could hear footsteps approaching.

He heard barking, too.

Suddenly the little round window in front of his face was filled with the snarling teeth of a killer dog. When the door opened a few inches, the teeth filled the gap level with Owen's throat.

"Don't mind him. He's very friendly," a man's

voice said. Owen could see a big hand straining to hold the dog's collar. "What can I do for you?"

Owen mumbled something about Japan, and tractors, and a calendar.

"A what?" the man said over the snarls and barking. "You'll have to speak up."

Owen tried to show him the 1939 yellow Farmall A, but the man wasn't able to open the door wide enough to see.

At the next house Owen was invited in by an old man who was very interested in the calendar. He used to be a farmer in the area, he told Owen. His hands shook while he talked, as if he were sitting on top of an old tractor in full throttle.

"You know, I used to have one of these," he said, looking at June's model. "I bought it new in 1926, I think it was." Then he looked at it some more. "No, no, it was '24 and I borrowed the money from my uncle Mort." He looked at Owen, the sagging skin on his throat shaking like a turkey neck. "Or was it Uncle Bart?"

He had pictures of his own tractors, which he got out to show Owen. The album was all black and had a thick cover with wide pages filled with old snapshots of many different pieces of farm machinery.

"This one here," the man said, "I bought at the start of the Great Depression, when everything was cheap. But I never had more trouble with a tractor. I swore this one had a will of its own. It was like a donkey let loose from the gates of hell. There was one time I got stuck in a ditch, and when I got off to try to free the wheels this demon lurched suddenly —"

The hands sped forward. Owen jumped.

"— and then I was trapped, you see, right beneath the wheel. Good thing it was muddy. I had a little room to slide and slither. And I was pretty thin back then." He looked to Owen like a bundle of sticks now. "I tried to sell her," the old man said. "But back in those days nobody had two nickels to rub together. If we didn't grow our own food we would've starved. Don't know what people would do now if those days ever came back. Hardly anybody lives on a farm anymore."

Owen said that he lived on a farm. Lorne honked the horn outside.

"So you're up at five milking the cows and doing your chores?" the man asked.

Owen said no, it wasn't that kind of farm. "We just live there," Owen said. The man went on to tell him all about the work that he had to do starting when he was four years old. He fed the chickens, and when it was thirty below the chickens came in to take over the spare bedroom.

Lorne honked the horn several more times and Owen thanked the man for looking at his calendar and telling him such interesting stories. The old farmer had stories of other tractors he had owned over the years, and Owen had a hard time making it out the door.

Back in the truck Owen said to Lorne, "I heard there were good families living on a street called River-something."

"That's a strange name for a street," Lorne said.

They drove around some more. Owen saw several houses that looked like they might need a tractor calendar, but he felt shy now and wasn't sure whether he should try them. It was getting late and he had sold exactly no calendars. He really wanted to try Sylvia's house, if he could find it. Lorne drove near the river but the streets were called Hainsworth and Meadowfare and Beamsbrook.

Finally, on a hill quite a distance from the river, was Riverside Place.

"1837 would be a good house to try, I think," Owen said.

"Really?" Lorne said.

He drove them slowly down the street until 1837 stood out like a beacon drawing Owen out of the truck and down the walkway to the front door.

It was a new house with shiny sides and an enormous garage. Somewhere in the back, Owen knew, was a swimming pool — frozen over possibly into Sylvia's own personal skating rink. At that very moment she might even be spinning like an Olympic skater in a fuzzy blur of impossible beauty. She had probably grown taller than him and wouldn't want to be disturbed.

Owen gazed back at Lorne in the truck. His uncle was looking at him to see what he was going to do.

So he tried to find the ringer. He searched all over, then finally opened the screen door and rapped with his knuckles. The sound seemed to be swallowed by the night.

Owen knocked again much louder, and then

louder still, and as he stepped back he saw the doorbell lit in red right in front of his eye.

Before he could ring it, the door opened, and Owen looked up at Mr. Tull.

"Good evening," Owen said formally. Then he cleared his throat. "I wonder if I might have a word," he said. He meant to pause and prepare himself to explain about the tractors and Japan. But his mouth kept moving. "With your daughter," he said.

"With my daughter?" Mr. Tull said in surprise. "Does she know you?"

"I think so," Owen answered. He thought of trying to correct his mistake by somehow indicating, briefly, the depth of his undying love. But he had no idea how to begin.

"Sylvia!" Mr. Tull called and stepped back from the door. Mr. Tull invited him in and asked his name.

"Owen Skye."

"Owen Skye," Mr. Tull said, rolling it around in his mouth as they stood together in the hallway. "That sounds familiar." Then he called out again, "Sylvia! There's an Owen Skye to see you!"

The house was enormous with white carpeting everywhere he could see, clean as fresh snow. The walls were white, too, and the ceilings had sparkles like gleaming frost. In the living-room was a fireplace ringed with shiny brass that nobody had kicked a dent in yet or even smudged. Nothing looked banged up or peeling or cracked or used in any way.

Sylvia came around the corner then, and Mr. Tull and the rest of the house fell out of Owen's vision.

She was not wearing a skating outfit but a white flannel nightgown, and her feet were bare, and her hair shone darkly golden, looking like it had just been brushed a hundred times.

"Owen?" she said. "What are you doing here?"

Owen dropped his calendars and picked them up again and then looked at her more closely. He felt as if he were standing at a fountain in the middle of the desert and had to drink as much as possible in a very short time. He tried to memorize the blueness of her eyes, the easy smile on her face, the slope of her shoulders and even the smoothness of the skin on her neck.

She wasn't taller than him at all. She was wearing a thin gold chain, which seemed exotic and beautiful.

And at the end of the chain, almost disappearing into the collar of her nightgown…

… was the copper wire ring that Owen had fashioned by hand and given to her when they had walked down to the river together the day she moved.

Owen managed to drop the calendars again.

She bent down and picked them up, and the ends of her perfect hair brushed against his snowy boots.

"What are these?" she asked, straightening up.

Owen swallowed hard and looked at her. "I came to give you a tractor calendar," he said, and thrust several at her at once.

She took one, delicately, and handed the others back, and then examined a September model that was pulling an enormous hay wagon.

"Well," she said in a puzzled way, and looked at him again.

"We're going to Japan," he announced, trying to sound authoritative. "I'm the vice-president."

"Of Japan?" she asked.

"I wrote you a Christmas card," he said, and

watched her eyes narrow into an unasked question. "But I forgot the stamp." Then, in mounting panic, he asked, "Do you like tiddlywinks?"

"Tiddlywinks?"

Without knowing how, quite, he was on the walkway, then running back to the truck.

When Owen was safely inside, Lorne asked him if he had been successful.

"Oh, yes," Owen gulped, stuffing the remaining calendars back into the box.

Lorne fired up the engine for the trip home. "So you sold one finally?" he asked.

Owen looked back to see Sylvia staring at him from the doorway, her features even at this blurry distance burning once again into his memory.

"What?" Owen asked.

WELCOME HOME

WEEKS slipped by and the class was no closer to Japan. Michael Baylor had to explain that the pen-pals who were all but confirmed were now less confirmed than before. But no one was to worry, because Michael Baylor's father had connections with another class that was almost certainly confirmed, and they would know within a few days. The letters to the unknown Japanese students had been composed before Christmas and said things like "I don't know what Santa will bring me," when in fact all those details were now quite known and almost forgotten. So Miss Glendon had them write new letters.

On Michael Baylor's insistence Miss Glendon kept a large chart marking how many calendars everybody in the class had sold. After a number of weeks Michael Baylor was up to nineteen, but no one else got past five. Owen's total remained stubbornly at one. He paid for Sylvia's calendar out of money from his own savings plus another dollar and a quarter that Horace had given him for cleaning out the garage.

Horace had never paid such high wages before. Owen thought he must have felt badly about making fun of the Japan trip.

But many people now seemed to be making fun of the Japan trip, and of Michael Baylor. It was hard to know how it started, but several days into the calendar campaign people began whispering, "Calendars! Calendars!" whenever he passed by, and his neck would turn hard red even when he was pretending he hadn't heard. Owen wanted to laugh, but it was not difficult to imagine that if he had given his speech first, he would now be the one trying to tell the class how to sell things door-to-door.

"My dad taught me how to do it," Michael Baylor said proudly, standing in front of everyone. "First of all, you have to be determined not to leave a house without selling at least one calendar. My dad taught me a little song to keep in my head. *One, one, one would be fun! But two, two, two are for you!*"

Titters spread through the classroom. Michael Baylor shifted nervously.

"Also, don't stand too far away from a customer," he said. "Lean in toward the door so it's hard for a person to shut you out." He leaned in toward them, and Martha Henbrock laughed through her nose until snot leaked out. "You need to have a good opening line," he said angrily, but then he couldn't seem to remember what his favorite opening line was.

"How about buy this stupid calendar and I'll stop bothering you!" Martha Henbrock blurted. Too many people laughed.

But no one had any better ideas for raising money. There were meetings and more meetings. Miss Glendon talked with Mr. Baylor, and a committee of parents was formed. They were supposed to meet on a Wednesday evening, but no one was free to come. So the meeting was postponed until the following Tuesday, and then the Thursday after that.

Neither Horace nor Margaret went to that meeting, but Owen heard from some of the others that difficult questions had been asked but not answered, that adults had shouted, that some people had left upset.

Miss Glendon called another meeting of the Junior Achievers Club, but this time she did all the talking.

"I'm sorry I let this go as far as it did," she said. "It was an experiment and I didn't want to hold you back, but I can see now that it was my fault that I didn't give you more guidance. I've apologized to Michael and I don't want to hear another person making fun of him or of the Japan trip. Is that understood?"

She was a serious person, like all teachers, but Owen could see there was something even more solemn about her now. The air felt thick as gravy. Michael Baylor sat staring at his fingernails. He didn't look so much like a president anymore.

"Is that *understood?*" Miss Glendon asked again. Murmurs fluttered nervously throughout the class.

"People who dream big dreams," Miss Glendon said, "who take risks for the sake of others, who do things out of the ordinary — we need to encourage, not make fun of them. Not shoot them down. Now I'm sorry that we aren't going to Japan. Frankly, it would have been a miracle if we had. But Michael had the vision and you supported it, and I wanted you to try to work together to have some good things come out of it. Even if we had just made contact with a Japanese class, that would have been something. Do you understand what I'm saying?"

There was a long silence. Owen thought he did understand. She was the first teacher he had ever known who admitted to making a mistake. It made her seem completely different.

"I'm sorry to say," she continued, "that Michael has told me he wants to resign as president. I can understand his feelings. I've asked him to stay on, to try to pull something positive out of this experience, but he has refused, which is his right. I think we have two options now. We could disband the Junior Achievers and forget about it. Or the vice-president, Owen, could step forward as president, and as a class we can discuss what we'd like to do next. We still have some money raised through calendar sales."

"Forty-two dollars," Michael Baylor said glumly from the back of the class.

Miss Glendon turned to Owen. She was asking him with her eyes and he felt strangely calm.

"I think Michael should stay president," Owen said immediately. "I think we should thank him for everything he has done, and have a big party — to celebrate the fact that we aren't going to Japan."

There was silence. Everyone looked at Michael who looked straight back at Owen. Michael's fingers tapped frantically, but Owen held his gaze until they stopped.

Finally Michael said, "I don't want to be president anymore." He smiled weakly. "I'd like to be vice-president, if that's all right. "I'd like to help out with the party but not be in charge."

Miss Glendon looked hopefully from Michael to Owen, from Owen to the rest of the class.

Finally Owen nodded and everyone started talking at once. They could use the money to buy food and drinks and decorations. Dan Ruck said he'd ask his father and uncles if they wanted to bring in their fiddles after all. Owen said he would ask his uncle to come in and teach them bird calling. He declared that everyone could bring in games, whatever they wanted. It would be this Friday afternoon so that nobody would worry too much about the details.

"We're going to be completely disorganized!" Owen said happily.

The work for the week fell away in the face of the preparations for the party. Owen kept expecting Miss Glendon to stop suddenly and say, "Now, we really must spend some time on long division," but she didn't. She seemed more caught up than anyone in buying the streamers and hanging them around the classroom, and making other decorations out of Styrofoam cups and paper plates and strings of painted macaroni. There were banners, too, brown paper signs that the children covered in layers of paint and then spelled out in giant letters, "Welcome Home!" and "So Glad to Be Here!"

Owen called up Uncle Lorne and asked him if he could teach bird calling at the party on Friday afternoon.

"In front of people?" he said.

"They're just kids," Owen said. "I'm their president and I told them you could come."

Lorne paused and finally said, "I can't. I have to work on Friday." Then he added, "But you're fine for the loon. You teach them that."

Owen gulped and went quiet. Finally Lorne

said, "You're all right in front of people. You'll be fine. Not like me."

Owen *was* all right in front of people. He found there was a special sort of nervousness that rushed through his body and made it exciting to stand up and say, "I think we should move all these desks over there!" and "Do we have enough cups for everyone?" just the way a real president would.

At one o'clock on Friday everything was ready. Tables sat full of chips and cheese biscuits, nearly overflowing the big bowls that students had brought from home. There were cakes and brownies, and too many cookies, and other big bowls full of cherry-colored pop and orange punch and brown sludgy cola rapidly going flat. In a rash moment Owen declared that the party couldn't begin until Dan Ruck's father and uncles arrived with their fiddles. As soon as he said it he realized how foolish it was. The fiddlers could surely join the party whenever they got there. But Owen didn't think that presidents were allowed to change their minds.

And so the class waited in awkward silence, with everything decorated and laid out. The games sat on tables waiting to be played, but everyone just looked at the door.

"Owen, is your uncle coming to teach us the bird songs?" Miss Glendon asked.

Owen somehow hadn't been able to tell the class that Uncle Lorne wouldn't be there. Everyone was looking at him as if it was his fault the party was ruined — with no fiddlers and no bird caller to go along with no Japan.

"Owen?" Miss Glendon asked.

Owen knew now exactly how Michael Baylor had felt with everyone's disappointment being packed into his own steaming neck.

"I'm not — " he said, but the words stuck. He coughed into his hand, and there was a gurgling sound, and he trilled just a bit to make sure his throat was clear. And then the unthinking part of his brain took over and in a moment he was standing in front of them all in full loon cry, his voice warbling through the room and gathering them all in. He closed his eyes to make it feel like he was back at the haunted house sitting on the red couch with night engulfing everything and the trees and the air so chilled and wild.

He sang out like a crazy, lonely, presidential

loon, knowing that no one in that classroom would ever look at him the same way again. His soul was opening up in front of them all. He didn't have a secret left in the world. He was letting his true voice soar and cry and reverberate in everyone's ears. They would all know everything about him as soon as he stopped.

So he kept on as long as he could, as long as his breath held out. He sang until tears streamed down his cheeks and the door opened and there were the fiddlers, as if he had summoned them.

Then he stopped and gasped for breath while everyone's attention was taken away.

Dan Ruck's father and uncles were tiny, gnarled, hard-skinned men. Miss Glendon went to greet them and help them set up in the cleared middle of the classroom, and she led the clapping and the dancing as if she'd been doing it all her life. She dragged Michael Baylor out first and then Owen and whirled them around and around the dizzy floor. In time everyone was organized with partners and groups, and they were all looking at their feet and counting steps here and there, and linking and unlinking arms.

It was sweaty, giggling, breathless work and

the more he danced the more Owen was filled with a surprising and saddening sense of regret.

As fine as this was, Sylvia wasn't there.

Sylvia was off in Elgin, where she couldn't hear his loon call, and couldn't stomp her foot to the fiddling, and couldn't see Owen being presidential. He closed his eyes and tried to summon her but he walked into an elbow instead and had to sit down and hold his nose.

Even this, he thought, would make a good story, if only she was here.

GLORIA PORK-PIE

"Is there someone special you'd like to invite to your birthday party, Owen?" Margaret asked as she served the beef stew. Steam was rising from the plates. Owen looked through it at everyone around the table, then ducked his eyes.

"Eleanor and Sadie, of course," Margaret said. "How about some of the boys from school?"

"Owen is in love with Sylvia Tull," Leonard said.

Owen stabbed a piece of potato with his fork.

"You shouldn't bother with love stuff at your age," Horace said, a chunk of mushy carrot hanging on his lip. "Save all that for when you can handle the misery."

"Horace!" Margaret said. "I think it's wonderful that Owen has an interest in such things."

Owen found he could breathe in but not out.

"Misery," Horace muttered again, and filled his mouth with sauce-soaked bread.

"Sylvia is in your class, isn't she, Owen?" Margaret asked. Her face seemed very bright, like that of a doctor who has extracted a heart from a chest and is watching it beat on the table.

"She moved away to Elgin!" Leonard chirped in.

"Did she?" Margaret asked.

Owen breathed out finally and stared at the food on his plate. He had climbed down from the drainpipe and seen the haunted house when it was invisible and become president and sung out as a loon in front of the entire class.

He could do this, too.

"I would like to invite Sylvia to my birthday," he said quietly.

"Wonderful! I am so looking forward to meeting her!" Margaret said. "We will all be on our best behavior." She looked particularly hard at Leonard.

"Well, Andy's in love with Eleanor!" Leonard blurted in such a loud voice that everyone jumped.

"Are you?" Margaret asked. Andy's face was so full of outrage he couldn't speak.

"They sat together at the haunted house and almost held hands!" Leonard cried.

Andy drove his fist deep into Leonard's bony shoulder. Then both brothers stood up and Leonard's chair toppled into a potted plant.

"Stop talking about me and Eleanor!" Andy roared. "You're in love with Sadie! She's always mushing up beside you!"

Before another blow was struck, Horace thundered to his feet.

"With me!" he said, pointing ominously to each of the boys.

"Horace —" Margaret said. But then her face clouded and it seemed she wasn't sure what to do.

"I need to discuss some matters with my sons," Horace said gravely.

He marched the boys up the stairs to the bedroom and closed the door and had them stand at attention in front of the bed while he paced back and forth.

"Gloria Pork-pie," he said to them. He looked each of them in the eye during a prolonged silence. "I used to be in love with a girl named Gloria Pork-pie." Leonard giggled and then looked guilty. "It wasn't her real name," Horace said. "Her last name sounded like Pork-pie but was something different. My father found out about her and called her Pork-pie and now after all these years I can't remember who she really was."

He paused and spread his fingers as if trying to grip the subject properly. "I was so in love with Gloria Pork-pie that my brain twisted around in my head. Everywhere I looked I saw her. She had red hair the color of autumn." He seemed ready to launch into a poem about her, but then he didn't.

"When you're young and have no ballast," he said, "love can hit you like a wave and knock you straight into tomorrow. You roll over and get sand in your mouth, and stagger to your feet. Then you get hit again and choke on the water."

He paced in silence. Finally he stopped.

"Any questions?" he said.

"Whatever happened to Gloria Pork-pie?" Owen asked.

"Precisely!" Horace said, with some excitement. "Whatever happened to her? My father sent me to camp for two months, and every moment I mooned over her. She got more beautiful and more intelligent and so special I couldn't bear the thought of life without her. When I got back and raced up the street to see her, there she was… Gloria Pork-pie. I couldn't imagine for the world what I'd ever thought was so interesting."

"Wasn't her hair… the color of autumn anymore?" Owen asked.

"It was just a dirty sort of red," Horace said. "She looked so ordinary I went up and stared at her to make sure she hadn't been switched while I was away. She thought I was crazy, and then she hit me."

Horace rubbed his bicep then as if it still hurt.

"At any rate, I hope that's cleared things up for you." He looked thoughtful for a moment, then left the room.

The boys stayed at attention for a few breaths, and finally Leonard said, "Sylvia Pork-pie." But before Owen could fly at him, his brother scampered out the door.

As the days passed, Owen didn't know if he should invite Sylvia to his birthday party after all. He could imagine Leonard calling out, "Sylvia Pork-pie!" as soon as she walked through the door. Horace would be all polite at first and shake her hand and then tell a dumb joke, and Margaret would keep offering her cake and ask her what her father did, and Sylvester would slobber her up and down. And Sylvia would look at the thinning brown carpet with the stain from when Andy had bled after trying to juggle pocket knives. She would see the marks on the walls from indoor baseball, the furniture that had been ridden by the boys when they were bronco-busters in a rodeo. She would miss her white carpets and her swimming pool.

And yet if he didn't invite her, when would he ever see her? He might simply start to forget her again — to lose the details of her and have Miss Glendon's face begin to replace hers as it had before.

He went into Horace's office and found Sylvia's telephone number, then dialed and asked for her in a voice that was as presidential as he could make it. Her mother answered and said that Sylvia was out. She asked who was calling and whether she might take a message.

"It's Owen. Owen Skye," he said.

"Oh, *Owen!*" she said.

"I used to be in Sylvia's class."

"Yes! And you came to her birthday party last year. I remember you." She said it as if she might never forget him.

Owen managed to tell Sylvia's mother the details of the invitation, and when he put down the phone he knew that a certain course had been embarked upon, and that he couldn't take it back.

Yet he could not quite tell his family that she was coming. When Margaret asked him if he had invited her he mumbled and looked away, and gave the impression that he hadn't really thought about it.

"Call her soon if you want her to come," Margaret pressed. "You mustn't leave it too late!"

Owen stayed quiet.

"We would all love to meet her," Margaret said.

"What's her name again?" Horace asked, and Owen fled the room.

The day of Owen's party was sunny but cold. It was spring now and most of the snow had gone but the ground was still frozen and summer seemed a long way off.

Margaret said to Owen, "I'd like you to wear something proper for your birthday." And then came the long, painful process of finding formal clothes for all the boys: blue jackets, white shirts, gray flannel pants, black socks and dress shoes that fit. She even forced them into ties, and Owen felt like it was all his fault.

"Why do we have to wear these strangle clothes?" Leonard muttered. "Nobody special is coming."

"Your cousins are coming," Margaret said. "I know you think they're special."

"But Owen didn't ask his girlfriend," Leonard said. "Sylvia Pork-pie," he whispered.

Owen glared at him, but Leonard was standing right next to their mother, looking ready to duck.

"Well," Owen said carefully.

"You didn't ask her, did you?" Margaret said.

"Well…" Owen said again. And then in a little voice he added, "I might have."

"What do you mean?" Margaret exclaimed. *"Did you or didn't you?"*

Owen meant to say that he did, but that he might have made a mistake — told Sylvia's mother the wrong time or the wrong address. Or perhaps her mother had forgotten to pass on the invitation. At that moment Owen couldn't quite believe that Sylvia Tull really was going to show up at his house in a little less than an hour.

"It's possible that she's coming," Owen said.

"Owen!" Margaret said. "You need to tell me these things. The house is… awful and I haven't finished the food." And she stormed off. It hadn't occurred to Owen that Margaret might be nervous about meeting Sylvia.

Margaret raced through the house rearranging the pillows on the chesterfield, and refolding the napkins, and pulling all the messy boots from the front closet and hurling them down the basement stairs.

"Sylvia Pork-pie is coming to Owen's party!" Leonard announced gleefully.

"Sylvia who?" Horace said.

Soon Owen found his brothers and his father lining the front window to watch for the arrival of the guest of honor. Sylvester seemed to sense that something was up and started sniffing and whining through the house, as if his special rock might have sneaked inside when he wasn't looking.

Owen ground his teeth and wished there was no such thing as birthdays.

At the sound of wheels on gravel Margaret ordered them all away from the window.

"Act natural!" she hissed.

Owen stood in the hallway staring at the door, unable to move. The bell rang and it was Leonard who flung it open.

"Happy birthday, Owen!" Uncle Lorne said and stepped in with a gift wrapped in green paper. Lorraine was with him, so large she could barely squeeze through the doorway. She hugged Owen to her huge belly. Eleanor and Sadie came in, too, wearing pink candy-floss dresses that made Owen wince.

What if Sylvia wore something like that?

"Owen's girlfriend is coming to the party!" Leonard called out. "Her name is Sylvia Pork-pie!"

Owen buried his face in his hands.

"Now we're all going to be very pleasant company," Margaret said in the general bustle of getting people in the house and settled. Owen considered bolting out the door and never returning.

But Sylvia was coming, and everyone knew, and there was no avoiding it.

When the bell rang again Margaret said, "Owen, dear, would you get the door?"

They all turned to look at him.

He forced his feet to move, and as his hand

was on the doorknob he imagined her, Sylvia Pork-pie, in a pink candy-floss dress looking ridiculous and forgettable.

He opened the door. There she was in a blinding silver coat — not her orange one that he remembered so well — with smart black pants and her hair tied back with a red ribbon. Her eyes were shy but still blue as the sky in summer. She had a small gift in her hand and she stepped right up and kissed him on the cheek as if they'd known each other forever.

Which they had.

Then Sylvester burst by him and leaped up, barking. His long slobbery tongue slurped across her reddening cheek, and two muddy paws imprinted themselves on the shoulders of her silver coat as she staggered backwards.

"Down boy! Down!" Horace yanked Sylvester by the collar. "Don't mind him!" he said. "He just gets a little rambunctious." Then to Owen he said, "Don't block the door there, son!" and Owen felt himself being pulled back just like the dog.

"Hello there, I'm —" Horace started to say, and then he switched. "Lee and Elizabeth!" he said. "I had no idea!"

Horace shook hands with his clients, Sylvia's parents, who were standing right behind their daughter.

"Come in! Come in!" Horace said. "We're having a party!"

"No, actually, we won't," Sylvia's father said. "We have to —"

"We're on the hunt for some new paneling for the rec room," Sylvia's mother interrupted. She looked nervously at the dog. Sylvester began to growl at her but Sylvia kneeled down and started stroking his neck and ears.

"What's all that?" she said, melting him into a quivering mass of friendliness.

Sylvia's parents kissed her good-bye and headed back to the car. Horace closed the door on Sylvester, leaving him whining and whimpering outside the house. Sylvia walked into the living-room with her eyes lowered. Someone had taken her coat.

Underneath she was wearing a simple white blouse, completely free of paw prints. On her ears were tiny, perfect pearl earrings. And around her neck, almost hidden in the blouse, was Owen's copper-wire ring on the thin gold chain.

"Have a seat, dear. It's so nice to meet you!" Margaret said, her smile stretched across her face like an elastic band. "I could just shoot that dog sometimes. Are you all right?"

"Oh, yes," she said. "I love dogs. I wish I had one."

Margaret pulled a chair for her into the middle of the rug and asked what kind of juice she would like.

The whole room seemed to hold its breath while Sylvia decided.

"Apple," she said finally.

She sat down and others arranged themselves. Even Leonard seemed to be awed into silence.

Margaret came back with a glass of apple juice and handed it to Sylvia, who seemed aware of all the eyes trained on her. Finally she took a sip, then looked around for a table upon which to place the glass. There was none handy, so she held the glass on her lap in both hands.

Then she gazed around the room again, her eyes moving more than her head.

"So, Sylvia. You used to live in the village, but now you live in Elgin!" Margaret said finally.

"Yes. That's right," Sylvia said, in clear agreement with the facts as stated.

Owen left the room then and came back in with the bowl of cheese biscuits, which he nearly dumped on Sylvia's lap while holding it out to her.

"Thank you," she said, choosing one biscuit from near the edge. She bit into it without getting orange cheese dust on her lips.

"It wasn't easy settling into a new school," Sylvia offered then. "I didn't know anybody and it was hard, at first, to make new friends."

"But you were able to," Margaret said, sitting down beside her. The horrible nervousness of the moment seemed to pass. Soon Eleanor and Sadie had pulled up chairs as well, and the four of them were talking about changes and friendships and how difficult it can be when you are the odd one out. Lorraine came by with trays of crackers and dip and paper plates and napkins, and Margaret told her to not do any work, not in her condition. But Lorraine didn't listen, and Margaret didn't leave her seat, she seemed to be so interested in talking with Sylvia.

Owen was still standing around holding the bowl of cheese biscuits.

"When is your baby due?" Sylvia asked, sounding just like a grown-up.

"Any day now," Margaret said for Lorraine. And then, again, she told Lorraine to sit down and stop making people nervous.

"I've always been late," Lorraine said, pulling up her own chair now, so that all the females were in a huddle in the middle of the room. Horace and Lorne had disappeared, and Owen didn't know what to do with the bowl of biscuits.

He took it back into the kitchen, finally. A few days before the party he had pulled out an old set of tiddlywinks, in case Sylvia might want to play. Now Owen led his brothers upstairs to set up the world's most difficult course. They used lamps and pillows and old shoes and all three family baseball bats as obstacles and traps, and ran the course right into the bathtub where the wooden tiddlywinks cup sat surrounded by scratched and stained white enamel.

It suddenly seemed extremely important that they should play and not think at all about the females downstairs who were so happy with themselves as company anyway.

Andy suggested they not take turns at all but

make it a race with everyone firing simultaneously. Owen agreed but almost immediately recognized his mistake. Andy had larger elbows and was able to use his big body to get in the way of a lot of Owen's and Leonard's shots.

One of Leonard's pieces fell into a running-shoe trap.

"You can't pick it up!" Andy said. "You have to shoot it out!"

"But it's stuck in the tongue!" Leonard said and knocked the shoe over. Andy charged him with a two-minute penalty. But after only thirty seconds Leonard threw his pieces down the hallway.

"I hate this game!" he declared.

Some of the pieces hit Andy on the side of the face and one bounced down the stairs toward the living-room.

In Andy's moment of distraction Owen managed to pull up to him and launch a few pieces ahead toward the bathroom. But Andy simply fired them back.

"You can't shoot my pieces!" Owen said.

"Of course I can!" Andy said.

Eleanor came up the stairs then with Sadie and

Sylvia just behind. Eleanor held Leonard's way-
ward piece.

"That's not how you play Tiddlywinks!" she
announced.

"We've made up a new version," Andy said.

"But there are official rules!" Eleanor said.
"You need a special mat. Play proceeds from the
corners with the pot in the middle. And you certainly cannot squidge another competitor's
winks."

"Squidge their what?" Andy asked.

"Their winks," Eleanor said. "That's the proper term."

"Well, I'm not squidging anything!" Andy
said.

Owen watched Sylvia take in the mess of shoes
and bats and scattered lamps on the floor, the on-
going argument, the red faces on Leonard and
Andy and Eleanor.

"Do you play tiddlywinks?" Owen asked her.

"Not really," she said.

"These boys don't either," Eleanor said. "They
don't know what they're doing!" And she marched
up the rest of the stairs, found the pot in the bathtub and then cleared an area in the hallway.

"The proper mat size is six feet by three," she said. "Leonard, can you find a yard stick?" Leonard went off as if ordered and came back in a moment with an old worn measuring stick from the kitchen. Eleanor used it to plot out a playing area in the hallway and placed the pot in the center.

"This will do," she said, "in the absence of a proper mat. We start with the winks in the different corners. Blue is always opposite red, and green is always opposite yellow. Now, we can play singles or teams. Singles play two sets of winks, and teams—"

"All these rules are ruining it," Andy said.

"No, they're not," Eleanor snapped. "They're making it better. What's the point of playing if you aren't going to adhere to the rules?"

A sound came from downstairs then that made them all turn. It was human, but just barely. It sounded sharp and wild and eerie, as if it belonged out on the river or in the woods.

No one said a thing, and then it erupted again.

It was from downstairs, and it was coming from Lorraine.

Owen heard Margaret say, "Oh, my God, is it now?"

All the children gathered at the bottom of the stairs and looked into the living-room where Lorraine was clutching her side on the sofa and Margaret was kneeling beside her.

"Get Lorne!" Margaret ordered.

Owen wasn't sure what he was doing. He grabbed Sylvia's hand and then together they ran outside down to the garage, Sylvester bounding beside them. Owen hadn't bothered with coats for either Sylvia or himself and felt the chill immediately. He didn't know how he knew that Lorne and Horace were in the garage.

But there they were throwing darts.

"Lorraine's sick!" Owen called out as soon as he saw them.

"What's that?" Lorne asked, his face suddenly ashen.

"Mom said to get you *now!*" Owen said.

Both men ran past them without another word. Owen found himself racing back to the house with Sylvia still holding his hand.

"She must be having the baby," Sylvia said.

When they got back inside everyone was

crowding around and it was difficult to see.

"Start the truck, Lorne!" Owen heard Horace say.

Lorne blundered past them and out the door.

Lorraine made more noises then, wild and startling, and Margaret said, "I'm not sure there's time to get to the hospital!"

"Of course there's time!" Horace said. "If Lorne doesn't take forever!"

But Lorne *was* taking forever. Owen waited to hear the roar of the truck engine but all was quiet outside except for Sylvester's worried barking.

"Go see what's taking him!" Horace ordered.

This time Sylvia dragged Owen out by the hand. They raced around the house and saw Lorne stretched out on the ice in front of the truck, not moving a muscle. Sylvester stood above him, still barking, but stopping sometimes to sniff and lick at the blood that was seeping from a gravelly cut on the side of Lorne's head.

So Owen and Sylvia ran back in and told Horace and Margaret that Lorne had slipped on the ice and wasn't moving.

"That's it! Now we *have* to go to the hospital!" Margaret said, and in a moment she and Horace were helping Lorraine out to the truck. All the children followed in the cold. Andy grabbed Lorne from under the armpits and tried to lift his heavy body, but only managed to raise him a few inches. Owen and Sylvia took the feet and Eleanor and Leonard grabbed the middle, but they still couldn't lift him.

Horace pushed them off. He kneeled down and cradled Lorne's bloodied head, then gently tucked his other arm under his larger brother's long legs. Owen watched his father close his eyes for a moment, then rise with one explosion of breath — *"Ha!"* — like a cork popping from a bottle. As if Lorne weighed nothing, Horace carried him to the truck and laid him down on the flat bed. Owen and Sylvia ran back into the house to get a blanket for him, and when they returned, Margaret was behind the wheel and Lorraine was sitting in the passenger seat, her eyes clamped shut and sweat dripping down her cheeks.

"You stay in the back with Lorne!" Margaret ordered Horace. "I'm driving!"

Owen thought Horace might argue, but he didn't say a word. In seconds he was kneeling beside his brother as Margaret gunned the engine

and the truck tires fired back gravel at the abandoned children who stood in shock, not even
waving.

Then the truck bounced up the driveway and
disappeared down the road, leaving the dust to
settle slowly.

MORE OF US

"IN a crisis, it's important to carry on as if all were normal," Eleanor announced when they were inside again. "Very soon, I am going to have a new sibling, but there's nothing that any of us can do to help right now. So we might as well continue with the birthday. Sylvia, will you help me serve the cake?"

Sylvia nodded while Sadie looked on, crestfallen.

"Oh, come and find the ice cream, if you must," Eleanor said to her.

All three boys went, too, to make sure the girls knew where everything was.

Eleanor said to Sylvia, "You're lucky to be an only child. It must be nice to have all that peace and quiet."

"Yes, it must be," Sadie muttered, and she stepped closer to Leonard when Eleanor gave her a dirty look.

Leonard said, "There was blood on the gravel where Uncle Lorne fell. I thought maybe his brains were going to fall out."

Sadie said, "I thought Mummy was going to die on the sofa."

"She left a stain," Andy said quietly. "She was leaking."

"Men are incapable of dealing with child-birth," Eleanor said to Sylvia. She had found the candles and was placing them on the cake. "Everyone must leave!" she announced suddenly. "Especially Owen! It's got to be a surprise!"

Owen returned to the dining-room where the big table and the extra card table were set elaborately for a crowd of ten. Margaret had folded the napkins so they looked like flowers spilling out of the glasses, and the silver cutlery shone atop the white linen tablecloth last seen at Christmas. Eleanor came out with the cake blazing like a comet and everyone sang, even Sylvia, who looked at Owen as if she wanted to tell him the funniest joke as soon as they were alone.

Owen had to blow four times to put out the candles, and when he finally pulled them out he counted thirty-eight.

They ate piece after piece, until the cake — a triple-layered, chocolate-frosted monster — was nothing but a few crumbs and smudges on the platter. Leonard and Sadie moaned on their backs on the floor, holding their bellies. Andy and Eleanor sat glassy-eyed on the sofa, looking out the window at nothing. Owen took Sylvia back into the kitchen where he sat her at the table and put a bowl in front of her and cracked an egg into it expertly, without breaking the yolk or spilling its guts on the floor. Then he let out a soft, romantic loon cry.

Sylvia looked on, at least a little bit impressed.

"What did you wish for when you blew out the candles?" she asked in almost a whisper, as if she didn't want the others to hear.

"Nothing," he said. And then he thought about it some more. "I didn't feel like I needed to wish for anything."

"You have a great family," she said. "I like them a lot." She looked at the egg in the bowl. "Everything's so unusual here."

"I hope Uncle Lorne is all right," he said, and the words started to pour out of him. "Last summer he married Lorraine. She used to be the widow Mrs. Foster and she would come by with these plates of cookies. Uncle Lorne would look like someone had just shot him in the throat and he'd run down to the basement. He used to live down there. Before he fixed it up it was so soggy we could hear the Bog Man gurgling. But now he's married. Uncle Lorne, I mean. So is the Bog Man, but then his wife died because of the radioactive bog minerals. It makes a difference."

"Radioactive bog minerals?" Sylvia said.

"Being married. Having someone to sit with you on the red couch." And she looked at him a dozen questions at once. "It's a long story," he said.

While he was trying to think of what else to say, she thanked him for the tractor calendar and Owen felt his face turn into an electric burner.

"I wasn't sure you would like it," he said shyly.

"I don't," she said with a sudden, big smile. "But thank you anyway. You were nice to remember me."

He wanted to tell her then that of course he would remember her, that she was burned into his bones and the back of his eyes and most of his brain.

After a time Eleanor divided them into teams for proper tiddlywinks, as she called it. Owen and Sylvia played together, and Owen missed nearly every shot because he was trying so hard to impress her, but it didn't matter. He was just happy to kneel beside her and watch her copper ring swing gently on its chain when she took a shot — squidged a wink, as Eleanor insisted. They played other games too: a snake-crawling contest in the living-room, with Andy as the trainer and Eleanor as judge, and then a Mount Everest competition that involved making it all the way to the boys' bedroom without touching the floor.

Eventually the clock drove round the afternoon. Then they all heard the sound of tires on gravel in the driveway and ran to the door for news.

But it was Sylvia's parents, come to take her home.

"Aunt Lorraine almost had her baby right here in the living-room!" Leonard told them. "Then Uncle Lorne smashed his head running for the truck and they've all gone to the hospital!"

"All the adults left?" Sylvia's mother said uncertainly.

"Did you see the blood on the gravel?" Leonard asked.

Sylvia's parents looked around at the coffee table in the hallway, the chesterfield cushions scattered in the living-room, the overturned lamps, the crumbs and plates and baseball bats, the crooked pictures on the walls.

"Why don't we just do a little clean-up?" Sylvia's mother said.

They all went to work while Sylvia's father called the hospital and learned eventually that Uncle Lorne was okay, but there was no baby yet.

Mr. and Mrs. Tull seemed like nice people, and they stayed to organize some dinner for everybody, starting with Owen's egg in a bowl.

Owen cracked more eggs, and Andy looked after the toast in the tricky toaster, and Leonard set the table. They were all squeezed around the kitchen table, eating and talking at once. It was strange to see Mrs. Tull buttering Leonard's toast and Eleanor passing the ketchup to Sylvia as if they were all part of a big, rambling family with a few different sets of parents, and substitute sisters and cousins who stayed for a while and then went away and came back.

Owen looked over at Sylvia and she looked at him.

And she changed in an instant.

She didn't turn into Sylvia Pork-pie. But she wasn't Sylvia the untouchable anymore either. She was Sylvia who spat out bits of egg when she laughed after Leonard spilled his milk, Sylvia who looked like she might have wanted to go home with Eleanor and Sadie and be part of a big gang for a time.

She was Sylvia who wasn't so hard to speak to, Sylvia who would have taken his hand and run with him all the way to the haunted house if only there weren't all these other people around.

After dinner and another clean-up, and some more games and phone calls, Horace finally came back in the truck. He thanked Sylvia's parents profusely and said that all was well, but there was still no news.

"Lorne has a concussion so has to stay overnight anyway," Horace said. "And babies… they come out on their own schedule, now don't they? I'm planning on getting a good night's sleep!"

Owen walked Sylvia and her parents to their

car. It was dark now and the wind was blowing cold blasts.

"You didn't open my present," Sylvia said suddenly when they were at the car.

"I completely forgot!" Owen said.

"Open it in private," she said. "You can tell me later."

Sylvester came bolting up to her from out of the shadows. Owen thought that he was going to leap upon her once more, but then he noticed that there was something dark and large in his mouth.

Something familiar.

"Sylvester! You found your rock!" Owen cried. But Sylvester ignored him and left the rock — it *was* the same one, Owen could tell in an instant — at Sylvia's feet.

"What's this?" Sylvia asked, and she kneeled down to pick it up. She didn't even seem to mind that it was coated with mud and slobber.

"He likes you. He's crazy about you!" Owen blurted. "That's his special rock that's been lost for months and —"

Sylvia hurled it then into the darkness and Sylvester galloped after it, wheezing with excitement. Owen took Sylvia's hand and wiped it clean on the sleeve of his coat.

Then Sylvia got into the car, and Owen couldn't see her for the glare of the headlights. He waved as they drove off, but he didn't know if anyone was waving back.

He walked slowly inside despite the cold.

"Sylvester found his rock!" he announced.

Eleanor and Sadie were staying the night. Horace said that since they were guests they would get the big bed upstairs and the boys could sleep in their camping bedrolls downstairs on the living-room floor. The girls didn't have nightgowns or toothbrushes and were not pleased about having to sleep in the boys' bed. But Horace rounded up some things from Margaret's drawer, and Leonard showed them where the crystal radio had been back in the fall when the fire broke out. There were still a few scorch marks on the walls, too.

"Maybe you don't realize how dangerous this room is," Andy said.

Owen found Sylvia's present and slipped down to the basement to Lorne's cot. He opened the wrapping carefully.

It was a box of special paper, with envelopes to match, and she had included a large sheet of stamps and another piece of paper with her name on it, *Sylvia Tull,* and her complete address, which he knew already.

Owen stared at the box with the blank paper. Then he turned it over. *Dear Owen,* she had written. *I miss your stories. Tell me what is happening.*

A pen fell out of the box then and bounced on the basement floor.

That night, as Owen was staring at the living-room ceiling in the blackness, with the stiff floor beneath him, the phone rang in the kitchen. Sylvester didn't bark, but made a muffled noise, as one would with a mouth happily full of rock.

Owen ran in the dark and got to the phone first.

"Hello!" he said breathlessly.

"Who's that?" a woman's voice asked. It was his mother—it had to be her—and yet Owen wasn't sure. He had never spoken to Margaret on the phone before, and she sounded different.

"It's Owen Skye," he said.

"Well, Owen Skye," Margaret said, "you can tell the others that there's now a Phyllis Skye as well. Your new cousin. She's six pounds, eleven ounces and she screams like a banshee. Mother and child are doing well. Tell the others, all right? You can all come visit in the morning."

Owen looked through the gloom at the kitchen clock, whose hands glowed in the dark. It wasn't quite midnight yet.

"She has the same birthday as me," he said.

"Yes, she does. Happy birthday, Owen."

Owen put down the phone. Andy and Leonard were standing beside him now, and Eleanor and Sadie had come down the stairs in their huge nightgowns, muffled forms in the shadows. Horace was still asleep. Owen could hear the snuffle and drone of his snores in the background.

"Well?" Eleanor said.

For just a moment Owen was seized with the desire to run past them, to gather Sylvia's special present and write it all down for her first.

But he couldn't stay quiet now, of course.

"There's more of us," he said to them simply, "and her name is Phyllis, and we'll meet her tomorrow."

Later, in the darkness once again, Owen

resumed staring at the ceiling. Occasionally head-lights from the highway carved a path across the window, which they never did in the attic bed-room. The whole house seemed different. Owen wondered if, when he woke up in the morning, he would be different, too. He was older now, after all. It felt like so much had changed.

Slowly, he took out all the morsels of the day and turned them over in his mind. The moments with Sylvia, especially, he let linger, until they became too much to hold. His eyes got heavy and he felt himself easing into sleep.

He would write her first thing in the morning, he thought. And he would meet Phyllis and write her about that, and there would be other things he couldn't even imagine, filling up tomorrow the way they filled up today.

Then sleep took him over and pulled him, in its steady and unfailing way, toward the great long river of tomorrows.